July 2016

To Doris —
Keep spreading the
Light!!!
Love &
Blessings!
Shellie

The Greatest Enchantment

A Forest Fairy Adventure

Shellie Enteen

authorHOUSE®

AuthorHouse™
1663 Liberty Drive
Bloomington, IN 47403
www.authorhouse.com
Phone: 1 (800) 839-8640

© 2015 Shellie Enteen. All rights reserved.

No part of this book may be reproduced, stored in a retrieval system, or transmitted by any means without the written permission of the author.

Published by AuthorHouse 09/03/2015

ISBN: 978-1-5049-4764-0 (sc)
ISBN: 978-1-5049-4765-7 (e)

Library of Congress Control Number: 2015914231

Print information available on the last page.

This book is printed on acid-free paper.

Because of the dynamic nature of the Internet, any web addresses or links contained in this book may have changed since publication and may no longer be valid. The views expressed in this work are solely those of the author and do not necessarily reflect the views of the publisher, and the publisher hereby disclaims any responsibility for them.

All characters in this book are a work of fiction. Any resemblance
to people living or dead is purely coincidental.

Cover illustration by Bill Oliver, Boy So Blue Graphic Arts

ACKNOWLEDGMENTS

Just as events in life have their own mysterious timeline, this book took almost 10 years to come to fruition. I understand now why there were extended breaks between bursts of creation—the story was given to me as I wrote it, and there were lessons to learn and patterns to release before I could properly scribe the ideas that would be given to me by higher, far-seeing forces. At the end of what are now the first 3 chapters, I thought it was done. Possibly, there'd be a sequel one day. But the time came when I knew it was meant to go on. I'm glad I listened to that urging, despite being in the flow of another writing project. I sincerely thank my Guides (or Muse, as some may prefer) for choosing me to deliver this piece, and for leading me to those things that would make me ready to do so.

All along the way, there have been synchronicities and signs to let me know I was on the right path. And all along the way, there has been the wonderful support I received from others. To them, I also want to extend my thanks.

Shelly Petnov-Sherman—for decades, my greatest and most encouraging 'fan'—agreed to read the story on a visit here and gave some wonderful suggestions. Cindy Hochman of "100 Proof" Copyediting Service, polished the prose with her editorial expertise, and gifted me with both her professional and personal approval. Rita Arrigo applied her practiced eagle-eye to the story; seeking and finding mistakes the writer never sees. And just when I thought an illustrator could not be found who would answer my needs in every way, I had the impulse to Facebook-message Bill Oliver, of Boy So Blue Graphic Arts. Working with him on the cover was as magical as his image has proven to be. Bev Shapiro, Louise Ballantine, Janis Levy, Raine Teel, Dr. Michael Wood, Joni Maki, and Carole Schaefer helped me keep the faith and carry on, with their suggestions and belief in the project. Loving family and other supportive friends have left too soon to hold this book in their hands and read my thanks.

Ultimately, when it comes to gratitude, it's impossible to follow the thread far and wide enough to acknowledge all the people and things that contributed to the making of even one of our daily meals. How, then, could it be possible to acknowledge all the things and people who, unbeknownst to them or to me, had a role in my being able to write this book? The best I can do is offer thanks and blessings to all the Beings…in every timeline, kingdom, and dimension…who made this book possible; and to you, the reader, for reading it.

Chapter 1

THE LAND THAT HAS NO FALL

It was Midsummer's Eve. In the green and flowering forests of the Blue Ridge Mountains, all the Fairies were preparing for the Great Festival that would be held that night. The air hummed with excitement. Of the four days that mark the gates of earthly seasons, Midsummer's Eve is the favorite of the Fairy Folk because it holds the energy of enchantment. On this night, after the festival and the proper ceremonies are observed, they fly off to further celebrate by casting temporary, and sometimes hilarious, spells on unsuspecting mortals. Each Fairy secretly hopes to bring back the tale of a spectacular enchantment; one that will be told again and again at future Midsummer gatherings.

As dusk deepened, all over and everywhere the door to secret cupboards in ancient oak trees sprung open to reveal a shining crystal bowl and polished acorn. Inside the bowl was the powerful, enchanting Rainbow Fairy Dust. Each Fairy placed a generous pinch in the gossamer pouch they tied around their waist.

The lids of the hollow acorns were removed and a drop of a special elixir stored inside was carefully poured into a thin crystal vial. This hung from the sparkling silver chain around each Fairy's slender neck.

Last, but not least, curled oak leaves unfurled, revealing chariots of spun gold. These were fastened onto the backs of waiting Fireflies for the trip to the Great Fairy Ring ... a perfect circle of giant white-capped mushrooms on a grassy clearing in the heart of an uncut forest, on the mountain now called *Grandfather*. The Ring was protected by an invisibility charm and could only be seen by the most sensitive and discerning mortal.

One of the first to be on his way to the evening's festivities was a handsome, gallant young Fairy called Runawind. Having plenty of time, he decided to stop for a moment on a shiny rhododendron leaf, next to a fluffy pink blossom that would shield him from sight. Here he thought he would practice his solo part in the Great Invocation Song just one more time. But, before he could begin, a wet drop hit his left shoulder, and then another, and one more, followed by the sound of a soft sigh.

He told the Fireflies to wait, and fluttered to the leaf above him. There he found the lovely, auburn-haired Melarose, hugging her knees. She was crying extremely large Fairy tears that left faint brown tracks on her silken beige cheeks. Her transparent wings of iridescent green were tightly joined behind her back. Runawind observed that the fine pattern of darker green veins that made the Fairies appear like fluttering maple leaves to unwitting human eyes were perfectly matched up; appearing stuck together, as though she might never fly again.

"Melarose, what's the matter?" he asked, with great concern. "It's Midsummer's Eve, the very best night of all! Why are you crying?"

Melarose just pointed at the trees around her and sniffled all the more.

"But, Melarose, the Festival is about to begin. They say Titania herself has come all the way from England to join us this year. Aren't you excited?" He certainly was. Even the tiny silver bells he'd had sown onto his best green tunic, just for this occasion, were stirred-up enough to jingle.

"It's just," Melarose began, but was overtaken with sobbing again.

"If you don't tell me, how can I help?" Gallant Runawind was really in a spot. He secretly wished he'd never stopped at that leaf, for now he'd probably be late and maybe miss his cue. But he couldn't very well leave Melarose there, crying all alone, could he? He tugged at the bottom of one of his small pointy ears with ill-masked frustration.

It seemed like an eternity passed, though it could have been just a blink of an eye in Fairy time, till Melarose said, "It's the trees, the leaves. I can't stand it! Once Midsummer's Eve comes, the days grow short and fall is on the way. Then the beautiful green forest will turn orange, gold, and red. The leaves will drop and the trees will be bare. Oh, it's just too sad for words!" To prove this, her crying began again, in earnest.

Runawind was truly puzzled. No Fairy he had ever known had ever expressed such a feeling. Every year since time began, the cycle of the seasons had followed their pattern of bloom and fruit and harvest and rest. But it was not the Fairy way to condemn another point of view. Nor was it gallant to leave a lady in distress, so Runawind thought and thought before he replied. And it must be said that, as he thought, he also hoped to find a solution as soon as possible so he could make it to the Festival on time.

For quite a while, Melarose cried and Runawind thought. From the corner of his eye, he saw the other Firefly chariots gliding by. Just when it seemed the whole night would pass this way, he suddenly remembered a story he'd been told at just such a Festival long ago. It was the tale of a Fairy who had journeyed alone to a place where Fall never came and Winter was unheard of. Where was that? Oh, why could he not remember? And then it came to him, like a whisper on the breeze. "South," he heard. "Go south, and then east, and you'll be there."

"Melarose!" He shouted so loud that passing Fireflies all lit up at once. His mop of carefully combed black hair bounced this way and that as he fluttered and hopped in front of her. "I know what we can do! There is a way to end your sorrow, and if you will just stop crying now and come with me, I'll tell you."

Melarose looked at him and allowed a few tearless breaths to go by. It was also not the Fairy way to lie, at least not to one another, so she knew he must be right. "Okay," she said. She stood up, straightened her tunic—in the flattering purple of the wild wisteria blossoms that dotted the greening forest in spring—gave her auburn curls a quick fluff, and extended her hand. The promise was made; the bond was sealed.

Together they fluttered down to his waiting Fireflies, hopped into the chariot, and were on their way. As they flew, Runawind told her why she would never be sad again. All her tears turned to dazzling smile-beams. They made a plan to journey south, and agreed that, since Fairies are less easily seen in the dark of night, they would leave a week after the Full Moon, which was very, very soon. They would find The Land That Has No Fall and, if Melarose wished, Runawind would help her settle there before returning home.

The Midsummer Festival was a big success, and Runawind was brilliant in his solo song. An especially moving speech by Titania, the glorious Fairy Queen, was followed by the ritual drinking of the elixir of immortality and hours of spirited song and dance, inspired by the music of a thousand Fairy pipes. Finally, with joyous enthusiasm, the Fairies prepared to fly off to sprinkle Rainbow Fairy Dust on the lucky creatures that would dream the special dreams of the Fairy realm this night. But, before they left, Runawind, having some serious doubts, if truth be told, thought he'd better see if he could find out more about The Land That Has No Fall.

Shouting his need into the Fairy-filled night, three Fairies finally fluttered toward him, saying they had information on good authority. And, so, he and Melarose were told about creatures never before seen and plants unlike those the Blue Ridge Fairies knew; plants that kept their leaves and stayed green all year. And a Fairy with wizened whiskers shook a finger at them to emphasize his point, and warned them about the lizards.

Apart from mortals, what a Fairy fears most are creatures with long, quick tongues who can mistake a Fairy for their usual winged food. In their mountain home, a frog or the occasional silly snake might do this, but there were very few lizards to meet up with in the Blue Ridge forest. Why, a Fairy could go a whole hundred years or more without running across a lizard and, even then, it would probably just be the wise Salamander. As a fellow Elemental, the Salamander certainly knew a Fairy when it saw one.

And it was true, all three Fairies agreed, that because of the numerous lizards, Fireflies refused to venture far into the South. Certainly they could not expect a Firefly chariot to take them all the way into The Land That Has No Fall. Melarose and Runawind had their own wings, of course, but a Fairy's wings are best used for fluttering and not for long-distance flight. They would have to find other ways to ease their journey.

Then Melarose asked a question that gallant Runawind had not even entertained. "Are there Fairies in The Land That Has No Fall?" Incantaro, the wise old wizard who was one of the three, gave her his most inscrutable smile and whispered, "The likes of which you've never seen."

Runawind was concerned by all he heard, but Melarose showed no fear. And, so, since a promise is a promise and a bond is a bond, the plan stood firm, even if Runawind felt a slight shiver despite the warm night breeze.

The week after the Full Moon came all too soon for Runawind, and not nearly fast enough for Melarose. On the very night, Runawind slowly strapped his chariot onto four Fireflies that had volunteered to take them as far south as they could safely go. Melarose fluttered about excitedly; making sure the Fireflies were in good shape for the journey.

Uncertain of what their next mode of transportation might be, they had decided to travel light. They took only a small amount of Fairy Power Juice, in light travel flasks carved from twigs of flexible green willow bark and covered with a network of spider web. Longer strands of web fastened the flask around their waist. To this, they also attached a small gossamer pouch of Rainbow Fairy Dust, just in case.

The crowd of Fairy friends who came to see them off wished them well. They were sure this adventure would provide many wonderful stories. Since all Fairies dearly love a good story, they could hardly wait for Runawind's return. They vigorously encouraged him to hurry and be on his way.

But the reluctant Runawind kept fluttering about, checking the chariot and talking with the Fireflies about the route, till Melarose finally said, "If we wait much longer, the Sun will be rising and we won't get far at all." Runawind had to admit that this was true and, so, amidst much waving and cheering, they began their journey.

The Fireflies carried them south for many days, or nights, as it were, and then came the moment they both were dreading. A tender pink sunrise had just begun when the Fireflies landed the chariot on a branch at the edge of a stand of trees. A different terrain stretched before them and they could see a number of plants that were not at all like those that grew in their mountain home.

With several rapid blinks of light, the Fireflies told Runawind that they would now return to the Great Forest. They had agreed to take the chariot back with them. Runawind and Melarose got out, put on their pouch and flask, and waved goodbye to their Firefly friends. When they could no longer see blinking Firefly light, they turned to face their future.

"What do you think?" Melarose asked.

Facing their direction of travel, Runawind pointed toward the left. "I see what appears to be a river. It should be flowing south. Let's go there and see if we can make a raft with leaves and twigs."

In the soft light of early dawn, the river looked closer than it was. Flying with a pouch and flask was a bit more demanding. When they finally reached the riverbank, Melarose begged to take some rest. Once they recovered some strength, they would look for materials to make the raft. Runawind selected the crook of a branch near the top of a tall pine tree. They settled wearily into beds fashioned from the fragrant needles.

As often happens, they slept longer than planned, and the sun was high overhead when they awoke. Melarose quickly fluttered down to a low branch and surveyed the river. She shot back upwards with a start when she saw a huge creature resting on the bank below. It looked like a lizard, but much, much bigger, with hard-looking skin.

"Runawind, come and see!" she called up to him. He was shocked, too, when he saw the enormous lizard.

"His tongue could probably reach for miles!" Runawind cried. But, just then, the creature opened its jaws and they could see that this was no ordinary lizard. Huge teeth lined the mouth, but no long tongue flicked out to catch the insects flying by.

"Look!" Melarose pointed to the river, where another of the huge creatures was swimming; its head, big eyes, and spiny back visible above the water. "Maybe this creature can ferry us down the river, if he will be so kind. Go and ask him."

"Me?" said Runawind. "I don't know their language!"

"All right, I'll go," Melarose replied, and fluttered down, landing softly on the creature's enormous snout.

"Hello! Good day! Are you planning to swim to the South, and would you let us ride for a while on your back?" she asked, in her best Universal Creature dialect.

"Hrrrrmmmphhh. Grrrrrmmmrrrrrgggglll. What?" the creature finally managed. "Who are you and *where* are you?"

"I'm a Fairy from the North." Melarose said. "And I am traveling south with my friend."

"Well, come around where I can see you ... don't have eyes on the front of my head, you know! Grrrrrrglllllmmmmmmffff," said the beast, and Melarose quickly complied. She fluttered in place, not far from his huge right eye.

"I see," said the beast. "You don't look very heavy. But I swim very slowly and sometimes I need to go beneath the water."

"That's okay," Melarose said. "While you are under, we can flutter above till we see you come back up. We'd be very grateful!"

"Don't know why you want to go south, but get your friend and let's get going! Grrrgmrfff Glargllllgllrrrp," he said, starting slowly toward the water.

"Runawind! Come right away!" Melarose called up to him. "We have a ride!"

Runawind looked skeptical, but Melarose said, "Come on! He's rough and gruff but very nice. We will just have to flutter above him once in a while when he goes underwater."

The giant lizard had already entered the river, and the Fairies hurried over, landing lightly on his back. The beast slowly swam to the deep water in the middle of the river and began his journey south.

Before long, they saw the homes of mortals lining both sides of the riverbank. Some were so high they blocked the light of the mid-morning sun. This, they agreed, was not so bad, as it was quite a bit hotter here than in their forest home and they were not accustomed to spending a long stretch of time out in the sunlight.

There were boats docked on the riverbank and people coming toward the docks with fishing gear. They were absorbed in watching this when the big lizard took his first dive. Fortunately, they managed to flutter up just as their feet touched the water. Fairy wings don't fare well when wet, which is one reason you don't find many Fairies flying about in the rain or swimming in ponds and puddles. They resolved to pay more attention to the lizard than the happenings on shore.

In a few minutes, the buildings stopped, the tree line began anew, and the beast rose up again. As they landed softly on his back, Runawind said, "I'll bet he goes down again the next time we see mortals." Shortly thereafter, Runawind was proven right.

This time, it was a bit longer before the lizard resurfaced. When they were quietly standing on the beast's back once more, a slightly breathless Runawind said, "I think this is going to happen more often than we thought. Do you have any suggestions?" They could already see the outline of more mortal dwellings in the distance before them.

"I guess we should make for shore at the next narrow stretch. We can find a place to hide until nightfall, and then build our raft."

But a narrow stretch was not to be found, and another extended flutter above the submerged lizard had them both quite exhausted. "I think I'll ask our friend to head towards the bank so we can take our leave," Melarose said, and flew over to the beast's right eye. As she did, the lizard lifted his head up from the water.

"Grrffmrgle grrrg," he said. "What do you want?"

"Please. We can see you are hiding from the mortals, and we certainly don't blame you. There seem to be so many here along the river! We are very grateful for the ride, but tired from all the flying, too. Can you please go closer to the bank so we can find a place to rest?"

"Grrrmmmgggrrrffflll," said the beast, as he turned toward the left bank. He stopped alongside a dock behind the lush garden of a huge white stucco home. On each side of the garden near the deck was a cluster of the odd-looking trees the Fairies had been seeing more frequently as they sailed down the river on the lizard's back. These had pale, slender trunks topped by drooping sprays of long, deep-green, pointed leaves that swayed easily in the slightest breeze.

"Thank you!" Melarose shouted at the great lizard, hoping he had heard this before he submerged once again. Then she and Runawind flew toward the trees, where they hovered uncomfortably under the sharp-edged, scissoring leaves, wondering what to do next. Clearly, they could both do with a sip of Fairy Power Juice, but the breeze, which had just picked up, made it hard to find a suitable place to land.

"Look—over there!" Runawind cried. Melrose gazed beyond his pointing finger and saw a large wooden birdhouse, atop a tall post nearby. Exhausted from fluttering against the wind, when they arrived, they were grateful to find the birdhouse empty. They agreed that a small nap was definitely in order, and fell asleep almost immediately. Outside, thunder rolled and rain began to fall heavily, but Melarose and Runawind slept on.

"Um-hmmm, Um-humm!" The sound reached them in their deep dreams. Runawind and Melarose awoke in the dimly lit birdhouse to see a large Dragonfly, with a bright green head and shimmering wings, hovering near the entrance. "I say, Um-humm! Might I come inside and rest for a while?"

Why, of course!" Melarose cried.

"Do you think a friend or two might join me? Um-hummm," the Dragonfly asked. Behind him, they saw a bright yellow Butterfly and two smaller Dragonflies of iridescent blue.

"I guess we can all fit in here," Runawind replied. "But why are you coming into a birdhouse? We were tired from our trip, you see...."

His words were drowned out by the humming sounds and beating of wings, until all four visitors had settled on the walls and floor of the birdhouse.

"The planes are coming," said the Dragonfly. His friends made small sounds of dismay.

"Planes?" Runawind asked. "Surely they can't fly this low here! Why, in our mountain home ..."

"No, it's not the planes we fear. It's what they drop from the sky," the yellow Butterfly said, flapping her wings.

"What do they drop?" asked Melarose, peering outside.

"Oh, you won't see anything," the Dragonfly said. "And you might not feel more than a slight touch, or not even that. But it's there, nonetheless, and it will kill us for sure. And it's not a pretty death."

With this comment, all four commenced to buzz and flutter their wings, in what could only be called a flying frenzy of fear.

"Okay, okay," Runawind said, trying to calm them. "But why do they do this?"

"They don't seem to know they are," the Butterfly said. "That is, they know they're dropping the poison, but it isn't for us."

"Who is it for, then?" Runawind asked.

"The mosquitoes that breed in the water left by the great rains and in the swampy lands nearby," the Dragonfly said. "The humans are afraid of them and don't like having to stay indoors at night. They want to kill all these biting insects."

"And, even though they don't fear us," the Butterfly cut in, "and even like to see us flying by, the spray from the sky catches all flying things in its deadly shower and affects us all the same."

Runawind turned to Melarose. "All flying things? That could mean us, too!"

"I should think so!" said the Dragonfly. "You'd best stay in here with us till the planes have gone and the shower has settled on the ground."

And, with that, the sound of a small plane's engine was heard, coming from the south. When it passed, Runawind asked, "How long do we have to wait?"

"We'd better stay inside till morning," the Dragonfly said.

As they all settled down for the night, the Dragonfly and the Butterfly spoke of all the things that had happened after the spray-planes appeared ... not just to them, but also to the birds and other insects, and even to the fish and frogs. It was such a sad story that Melarose began to cry. This was deeply disappointing, as she had thought she would never be sad again.

Runawind intervened, trying to stop her tears with more information. "I'm sorry to hear all that ... but, how often do the planes come?"

"Oh, they won't come again for a while now ... maybe a moon or so ... and then not so much when the rains stop and it gets a bit cooler," the Dragonfly replied.

"And how did you know they were on their way?" Runawind continued, thinking the information would be helpful for his friend.

"I guess you didn't see, since you were in here sleeping," said the Butterfly. "But a big band of insects flew by, getting as far away as they could from where the spraying began. We find out about the planes from those who manage to escape and warn us."

"There," Runawind said to Melarose. "It doesn't happen often, and you will know before it does, and then you can find a place to hide!"

But she looked up at him with big tears in her eyes and he knew that somehow this idea was not reassuring.

"Well, since we're all here for a while, I can sing a bit of our Invocation Song, and we can tell some stories to pass the time," he said. But, as he spoke, he saw that the four flying ones had already fallen into their form of slumber. He looked at Melarose. "I'll sing for you, if you like."

"It's okay," she said, wiping her tears away. "I'm fine. Let's get some rest so we will be able to make our raft in the morning."

And, so, another night passed, though neither Melarose nor Runawind slept very much at all. And certainly their eyes were open wide when, at dawn, the Dragonfly woke and began to fly about the birdhouse. His buzzing drone soon woke his friends and they too began to flap and fly about.

"Thank you for sharing this shelter with us," the Dragonfly said, as the four prepared to leave. "Stay out of puddles, if you can, and don't drink any water for a day or two!" he cautioned, and followed his friends out the opening.

"Okay," Runawind said, waving goodbye. He turned to Melarose. "I guess it's time we were on our way, too."

With little enthusiasm, they ventured out of the birdhouse and pondered their mission of collecting bits of leaves and twigs.

They realized that the foliage would be covered by a mist of poison, and thought they had better devise some other plan. They fluttered slowly through the lush landscape, which now appeared more hostile than beautiful.

"This may be far enough south anyway," Melarose said listlessly.

"Look there! That could be a good place for you to settle," Runawind said hopefully, as they came to a gazebo lined with potted plants of all sizes.

They entered the structure and stared, mesmerized by beautiful multicolored blossoms that bloomed along a slender stem. They were the most attractive flowers Melarose and Runawind had ever seen.

"Orchids!" a high-pitched, haughty voice called out. "This is my home, by the way, and you are, technically, trespassing."

Runawind and Melarose looked around to find the speaker, and there, beneath the large green leaf of a flowering peace lily, they saw a most amazing sight. They flew closer to take a good look. Yes, they thought, this must be a Fairy, though he was very, very different, to be sure.

"Don't flutter there, gawping at me! Have you no manners?" the Fairy said, clearly exasperated.

"I'm sorry," Melarose began. "It's just that we are far from home and have never seen a Fairy quite like you before."

With this, the Fairy seemed to swell with pride. "Of course not!" he exclaimed, and with a great deal of effort, began to move his unusually large wings. He could not lift himself far, and made little tapping sounds when his toes kept touching back down on the wood of the bench below him. His lips were swollen into a perpetual pout and he appeared to have blue circles painted around his eyes. Jewels the size of dew drops hung from his ears, pulling the lobes down so far they almost reached his neck. "Country bumpkins like you would not know the latest in fashion!" he declared in a condescending tone, as they gaped at him.

"Fashion?" asked Runawind. "What's that?"

"Ha!" the Fairy snorted. "Never mind."

"But how did you get those large wings …who painted your eyes … why are your lips so big … and your ears?" Melarose was beside herself with curiosity.

Tired of the effort, the strange Fairy came to rest, and motioned them to join him on the bench. "So many questions! Name's Arnold, by the way."

"Arnold? But that's a mortal name, isn't it?" Melarose asked.

The Fairy sighed at her ignorance. "Fashion, like I said. Most of us changed our Fairy names long ago. And most of us look like this, too … you'll soon find out … and then you'll want to do the same. To fit in, of course, and be admired."

"Still—how?" Melarose pressed on, while Runawind stood silent, clearly disapproving.

"Several charms, a few potions," he said vaguely, then engaged happily in what appeared to be his favorite topic. "As for the wings and lips, you must go to the right Fairy Fixer, though … I've heard awful stories about botched jobs … one wing bigger than another, lopsided lips…." Melarose took a sharp intake of breath, so he paused for dramatic effect. "Never mind," he continued, finally warming to her seeming interest. "I will tell you who I use."

"Never mind is right!" Runawind shouted. "What good is it to be a Fairy and not be able to flutter up to the treetops or fly off to sprinkle Rainbow Fairy Dust? Whoever thought of those wings should have their head examined!"

"But, Runawind," Melarose began. "One good thing about the fat lips and big wings—I'll bet the lizards don't think he's food." She finished with a silvery giggle, which just seemed to fuel Runawind's irritation even more.

"Come on, Melarose! We should leave the home of Mr. Arnold Fairy and be on our way."

Chapter 2

A SERIOUS ENCHANTMENT

At that precise moment, a large lizard darted from behind the potted lily and appeared to disprove Melarose's theory by lassoing Arnold with its long tongue. The more agile Melarose and Runawind fluttered quickly away.

"Bet that lizard has a hard time digesting the earrings," Runawind said gruffly, as they flew toward the entrance to the gazebo.

"Oh, that's not kind at all!" Melarose said, clearly distressed.

"I'm sorry; it's just that the whole Fairy Fashion thing has me a bit peeved," he explained. "I'd hate to see you do those things to yourself just to fit in with the Fairies here."

"I know," Melarose said softly. "I'd feel the same about you."

"Wait! Wait!" They turned and saw Arnold standing on the bench, next to the large lizard, waving his arms at them.

"Arnold?" Runawind began, but Melarose was already fluttering back. She stopped a cautious tongue-length away and hovered, waiting.

"Please, please help me—er, us, I mean," Arnold began. The large lizard crooked his head and looked up, as Runawind joined Melarose.

"Okay, Arnold." Runawind sounded suspicious. "Just what is going on here?"

"Well, er, that is, you see ..." Arnold stuttered.

"Out with it!" Runawind shouted so loud that Arnold jumped.

The Greatest Enchantment

"Okay, okay! The thing is, this is no ordinary lizard," he sighed. The lizard lifted his head higher, with what seemed like pride.

"It isn't?" Melarose asked.

"You were right," Arnold admitted. "Part of the reason we all had wing augmentation and lip enhancement was to be too big for a lizard's meal ... or a frog's, for that matter. You know, we have some very large . . ."

"Enough, enough! We can't flutter here forever!" Runawind's impatience with Arnold was growing by the minute.

"Yes, yes. Anyway, this lizard ... rather, Jack here, is not a lizard at all. That is, he is now, of course, but he wasn't always."

"So, then, what was he?" Melarose asked.

"He is the owner of this house ... of this very gazebo, in fact. And he was enchanted on Midsummer's Eve by a group of Fairies who thought that his nature was best reflected in the lizard essence." Arnold sighed again, while the lizard gave them all a squinty sideways glance that held more than a little malice. "He agreed to let me go if you would return him to his former human state."

"What makes you think we can do that?" Runawind demanded, ready to leave Arnold to his fate.

"I see you have pouches around your waist ..." Arnold ventured.

"But we have just enough for a sprinkle or two," Runawind said, turning to go. "Not nearly enough to reverse a serious enchantment like this!"

The lizard flicked out his tongue and grasped Arnold around the waist again.

"Oo ouch ... my wings!" Arnold cried. "Please, please ... can't you do something?"

"There is a way, perhaps," Melarose said, more to herself than to anyone.

"What?! What?! Please tell me, er, him!" Arnold began crying. The blue circles around his eyes were now running in stripes down his cheeks.

"Well," she began, looking at Runawind. "The Fairy Dust we have might return him to his mortal state, but it would only last for a few hours or so. Then he would turn back into a lizard. But we could ration it out to make it last a couple of days, or at least long enough to get back to the Great Forest."

"Back? What are you thinking?" Runawind was definitely not happy with this idea.

"If we can get him back to the forest, Incantaro and the Circle of Seven can help."

"But why should we do this? Why bring this lizard into our forest home?" He was not at all sure that Melarose was thinking clearly.

"I don't know," she pouted prettily. "I just feel we should. And …" She paused, as her own eyes filled with tears. "I want to go back, too. Maybe he can help us get there."

At this, Runawind brightened, in spite of himself. "You want to go back?"

"Yes. I do."

"Great! Okay!" He suddenly filled with enthusiasm.

"Thank you, thank you, I really do thank you," Arnold said sincerely.

Runawind turned to him. "I'm not doing this for you," he said. "Not for that lizard either."

Runawind and Melarose looked at each other, and some new feeling passed between them.

"Okay, then." Melarose said softly. "Let's figure out how we'll manage this."

Several hours and a few drops of Fairy Power Juice later, they hit upon part of a plan. They would use a small amount of Fairy Dust and invoke a special incantation that would make Jack human again for a few hours. He would then be able to get things ready and they could start the drive back to the Great Forest. They reckoned they had enough Fairy Dust to work the temporary charm three times. But, sadly, this was not enough time to get them back with Jack driving, and what of the downtimes while Jack was back in lizard form? Clearly, they would need another driver. And it had to be someone they could trust with the secret, too. This had them all stumped for a while, until Arnold finally piped in.

The Greatest Enchantment

"Oh! Of course! I have the perfect person!" He fluttered and tapped excitedly. The lizard turned a beady eye on him.

"Next door. The girl who takes care of the tropical birds. She comes from the mountains to the north, and I believe I heard she might want to go home for a visit."

Runawind and Melarose eyed him suspiciously.

Arnold stood up straighter, disdainfully turned up his nose at their questioning attitude, and intoned, "I have friends who live in the trees near the patio where the birds are kept. They told me. She can see them, too."

"That's unusual," Melarose offered.

"Yes, she talks with them as though they are her friends," Arnold said, becoming excited again at this prospect. "One time, she came here and we spoke for a little while. Lovely girl ... let's go and see if she's around. I'm sure we can get her to talk with Jack here, too, once you have made him human again."

"Just stay here," Runawind said to Jack. "Come to think of it, you stay, too, Arnold; it would take us days to fly to the next garden with you along!"

Melarose couldn't help letting a silvery laugh escape. This time, Runawind was delighted by the sound. She was going home. With him! The idea made him feel like he could accomplish anything.

They flew quickly to the trees Arnold had described and found a small cluster of Arnold-like Fairies standing on a branch together. Apparently aware of their approach, they eyed the Northern Fairies suspiciously.

"Who are you?" the largest one yelled, as they came closer. "You're not from around here—I can see that!"

"Settle down," Runawind said, secretly amused, while the Fairies on the branch made the same dismal attempts at fluttering that Arnold had.

"We are friends of Arnold's," Melarose soothed. "He's been captured by Jack, the, um, lizard. He asked us for help."

The flutter–flops became more agitated, and several Fairies let out groans of distress.

"It's okay. Please don't worry," Runawind quickly said. He felt he'd be unable to contain his laughter if their agitated attempts to become airborne continued. "We have a plan to help Jack that will save Arnold, too. But we have to meet the girl who takes care of the birds here ... your friend."

"Lily White Dove?" the first Fairy asked.

"If that's her name," Runawind replied, a tad sarcastically. Melarose gave him a cautionary look.

"Well, you're in luck then," the Fairy said, "because here she comes now!"

And, in fact, there was a lovely young woman with long black hair walking slowly across the patio toward the trees, carrying a large shell and a long, brown-and-white-striped turkey wing feather. As she came closer, they could hear her humming softly. Her smile sent out ripples of pink and purple light, and her song seemed somehow familiar. It made them want to dance and sing along with her. Some of the Fairies around them started to do just that.

Lily stopped and placed her shell on the glass top of a white cast-iron table. Then she reached into a small, brown leather pouch she wore around her neck and took out some loose tobacco. She offered it to the sky and earth, touched it to her heart and lips, and then sprinkled it on the ground in front of her. Striking a match, she fired up the herbs inside the shell bowl. Singing a different song, she lifted the shell and drew the feather slowly through the rising plumes of fragrant smoke several times. Then she used it to direct the smoke to the north, east, south, west, up to the sky, down to the earth, and then toward herself. She drew the feather through the smoke again, then placed it and the shell down, and began praying in a soft voice. It was a prayer of gratitude, which made the Fairies draw closer to bask in the gold and pink light around her. When she finished and opened her eyes, Melarose and Runawind were hovering right in front of her, but she didn't seem startled, or even surprised.

"Hello," she said. "I am blessed to see you."

"Oh," Melarose sighed, enjoying the rosy ripples that came with her words.

"And we are glad we found you. We have to ask an important favor. It's for a friend who needs help," Runawind said, grateful that Lily seemed to understand every word.

"Arnold?" she asked.

"How did you know?" Melarose fluttered a bit closer. Lily held out her hand and Melarose settled onto the palm. Runawind alighted next to her, on the tip of Lily's thumb.

"I had a dream last night that Arnold was in trouble. It's about Jack, the man next door, isn't it?"

"Why, yes," Melarose said. "Jack was turned into a lizard by some local Fairies, and he is holding Arnold hostage till he can get someone to turn him back into a human being again."

Lily sighed. "Well, you can turn him back into a man, but I wonder if you can turn him into a human being."

"What do you mean?" Runawind asked.

"Jack's a two-legged in male form. That is, when he's not a lizard." She laughed. "But it takes more than that to make a human being. I wonder if he has the qualities inside that would give him that nature." She laughed again. "I can see why the Fairies chose lizard!"

"Why?" Melarose wondered.

"Jack made his fortune from building expensive houses, like the ones here, on this strip of land on the beach side of the river. Then he and his partner built large communities further inland, in an area that used to be swampy wetlands. He had that land filled in, putting homes on places that could sink down one day. That area had been the home of animals and birds, and people without much money who had nowhere else to go or had grown up in generations, living on the land. Drying up the wetlands changed the weather pattern, too, so we have less nourishing rain, more big storms, and many more tornadoes. It would take a cold-blooded creature to do something like that—a creature that didn't care about anything but himself."

"I see," Runawind said regretfully. "But we promised to take him back to the forest and have the spell broken by our wizard. And we have only a little of our Fairy Dust with us, and that won't work for long. So," Runawind began, and then fell silent.

Lily looked confused. Melarose spoke up. "We need someone to take us up there; someone we can trust with the secret and who won't be upset when Jack turns back into a lizard every now and then. Arnold picked you."

"I understand now. I'm honored by his trust," Lily said softly. "But I must pray on this and ask if it is right. I hope you understand. I promise I will come to you with my answer, either way."

Runawind scowled, but Melarose replied, "Of course we understand. It has been a pleasure to meet you, Lily White Dove. Come along now, Runawind ... oh, and I am Melarose!" She smiled her sweetest smile, and fluttered up from Lily's palm, with Runawind close beside her. "We will wait for you in the gazebo." As they flew off, they heard Lily begin her prayer-song.

"Well? What did she say?" Arnold cried, when he saw them approaching the gazebo. He tried to flutter, but Jack had a claw clamped on his right foot.

"Do you hear her singing?" Melarose asked. "She is asking for guidance. She will come and tell us, either way."

Jack's lizard eye glared. "I can understand why she has to ask," Melarose said to him sweetly. "Apparently, you aren't very nice as a man either."

The lizard hissed and his tongue darted, forcing Melarose and Runawind to move quickly backward. "Take it easy!" Runawind said, landing on an orchid stem. "That attitude might have worked for you before, but it won't help you now."

Just then, they heard the singing stop. They all turned toward the pathway that would lead Lily to the gazebo. In a few moments, they saw her coming toward them.

"Hello, Jack," Lily addressed the lizard. "You have been given a big opportunity, though you don't realize that now. And you have met some wonderful friends." She gestured toward Melarose and Runawind. Turning to Arnold, she said, "Do you see why your natural Fairy wings were better than the ones you have now?" Arnold blushed and turned his eyes away, a big tear creating another smear of blue. "It seems it is a day of truth for us all."

Runawind fluttered to Lily's side, looking a bit puzzled. Lily just smiled. "During my prayer, I was told that I had been given a chance to go back home, to my family, to help preserve the old ways."

"Home?" Melarose asked.

"Like you, lovely Melarose, I left my mountain home to seek something different and, like you, I found little to be gained, and much to lose, by doing so. But I clung to my decision. I didn't want the ones at home to see me as a failure. I even had a crush on the dashing Jack here, and hoped one day he would notice me."

The lizard stepped forward, releasing Arnold's foot, and tilted his head. "Yes," Lily said. "Even though I knew what kind of man you were. I thought I could change you." She smiled. "The foolish thought of many women. But, look, someone did change you after all!" she laughed. The lizard glared. "I'm sorry," she said. "That wasn't kind. I will try to do better."

"Does that mean ..." Runawind began, settling down on Lily's arm.

"Yes, it means I'll go with you, help Jack, and return to my people. I'm sure we will all understand more as our journey unfolds."

"This is wonderful!" Runawind exclaimed, and Melarose nodded her agreement. They looked at each other and back at Lily. "But how do we proceed?"

"You say you have enough Fairy Dust to turn Jack back into a man for brief periods?" Lily asked.

"Yes," Melarose replied.

"Then I suggest you all wait here while I get my things ready and ask my employers for a leave of absence. I'll let them know I've been asked to drive Jack's car somewhere and that I need to leave today, and hopefully, right away. They're kind people and they will understand. I know someone who can look after the birds, and I will contact her too. When I return, you can give Jack enough time as a man to give me his car keys and a credit card, and to pack some things of his own. How does that sound?" Lily asked.

"Sounds good to me," Runawind said, and saw the lizard nod his head in approval too.

"Lily, Lily!" Arnold cried. "How can I ever thank you?"

Lily just smiled. "Return to your true nature, as I am doing. And help your Fairy friends remember their purpose."

"Our purpose?" Arnold asked. He truly seemed to have no idea what that might be.

"You are the joy of the natural world," she said softly. "The laughter in the waterfalls. The great peace of the swaying trees. The love in the scent of the blossoms. You inspire growth and balance the elements. Without you, our world is a sad and sorry place," she concluded, and turned to go.

"Oh. Yes." He blinked hard several times. "I remember now," he said, removing the jewels from his earlobes, which allowed them to spring back up to a reasonable level, and smiling the first real smile Melarose and Runawind had seen. And, in response to his true Fairy Smile, the palm trees began to sway and the aroma of blossoms filled the air. "Yes!" he cried, noting this. "It's like I've been asleep, but I'm awake at last."

Lily looked back over her shoulder. "I see good things are already coming of this." She smiled again, and disappeared into the next yard.

For Runawind, it seemed an eternity until Lily returned. He watched the lizard pacing the bench, and listened to Arnold puzzling out how he and his fellow Fairies had fallen under the materialistic spell of the mortals and what they must do now to get back to their former selves.

"I wonder if this wing augmentation is reversible," he heard Arnold say, as Lily finally came into view. She was rolling a red suitcase that bumped along over the grass behind her and she wore a blue backpack that was stuffed to the seams. When she reached the gazebo, she stood quietly, waiting.

"Oh!" Melarose was startled. She too had been mesmerized by the lizard and Arnold's non-stop talking. "Come, Runawind, let's get to work on Jack."

"Don't use too much," Runawind cautioned, as they hovered over the lizard, opening their small pouches and reaching in for a tiny pinch of Rainbow Fairy Dust. They sprinkled it on his scaly spine while they sang the ancient Song of the Forest and called upon wizards of long ago and their good friend Incantaro, asking for their help in reversing the spell. Finally, they spoke some words known only in the old Fairy tongue, and with a sudden *pfouuuffff*! Jack appeared: a lean, handsome, brown-haired man sitting on the bench. He was still wearing the designer jeans, white silk shirt, gold chain, and Rolex watch he had on when he was turned into a lizard. He stared at his hands, unable to speak.

"Jack, we haven't much time," Lily said softly. He looked up at her. She reached over to help him stand. "You'll be fine," she soothed. "But if you need me, just call out."

"And don't think you are reversed for good," Runawind said, reading Jack's mind. "You won't have long before you will be a lizard again."

At this, the still-silent Jack released Lily's hand and began to walk toward his house, gingerly at first, then gaining speed. He vanished into the doorway.

"While we wait for Jack, please tell me where we're going," Lily said, sitting down on the bench Jack had vacated.

Runawind looked on, smiling, while Melarose told Lily all about the wonderful forest on Grandfather Mountain and the special wizard who would reverse the spell. As she spoke, Melarose realized how much she longed to be back there. She even told Lily how beautiful the trees were when their leaves turned colors. She heard herself describing Winter, too; the brushstroke patterns made by bare tree limbs, the sacred stillness as plants slept under the cold earth, the calming presence of the evergreen pines, the crimson-colored cardinals foraging for berries on snow-covered branches. When she finished, she looked at Runawind, who fluttered to her and took her hand.

"There he is," Lily said. And, sure enough, there was Jack in the doorway, with two large, tan leather suitcases.

"Come to the garage!" he called out to them with urgency. Apparently, he was taking the timing seriously. Lily laughed and started away. Melarose and Runawind turned to Arnold, who seemed filled with mixed emotions.

"How can I ever thank you?" Arnold said. "I'm sorry I can't come along. But there's a lot to do here to get things back to normal."

"You can do it," Runawind said sincerely. "And we have all gained from this meeting." He looked at Melarose.

"We will always remember you, Arnold," Melarose said. She sent him bursts of smile-beams, and then turned to go.

"If you're ever down this way again, do stop by!" Arnold called, as they fluttered away.

"Not much chance of that," Runawind muttered. Still, he had to admit that if it weren't for this trip, and Arnold's predicament, his own future might not look as bright as it did now, with Melarose at his side.

When they entered the garage, they found Jack giving Lily explicit instructions on how to drive the monstrous black Hummer. He described how to use the navigation system, as Lily unzipped her backpack and took out a large sky-blue beach towel. She spread it on the beige leather passenger seat.

"What's that for?" Jack asked impatiently.

"You will be more comfortable on this. It has more grip for when …" she started.

"Okay, okay. Very thoughtful," he begrudged her. "Well, let's get going. No time to waste!" He got in the car, and motioned for her to do the same.

Lily stepped up into the driver's seat, putting her backpack between them. "There are a few things in here I may need," she said, to Jack's questioning look. Making sure Runawind and Melarose were safely inside the car, she started the engine and backed slowly out of the garage.

"Button on the visor," Jack offered. He watched the garage door close silently, as they backed down the driveway. "How much longer do you think I have?" he called to the Fairies, who were tucked between the suitcases on the back seat. They were not used to riding in cars, and felt a bit safer this way.

"There is no real way to tell, but I'd say you have only a short while before you start to transform," Runawind said.

Jack groaned. "Ever been a lizard?" he asked Lily, in a gruff attempt at a joke.

She gave him a patient smile. "I'm sorry, Jack. But you'll be returned to yourself soon. In the meantime, is there anything else you want to say?"

The Greatest Enchantment

"I'd like to know what you said about me to those Fairies," he answered.

"In due time. But I'll have plenty of time to talk to you ... this is your opportunity to talk to me," she pointed out gently.

Jack shrugged, some of the coldness starting to melt. "Of course, you're right. I need to say thank you." He ran a hand through his hair. "Not easy for me. But, believe me; I know how lucky I am that you were living next door."

Lily accepted this without a word and began to drive north on the beach road that ran in front of the homes. She looked over at the ocean, which seemed so tranquil today. "I'll miss the beach," she said. "But I look forward to seeing the mountains again. They say "permanence" and "peace" to my heart. The ocean's moods shift and I shift with them. It was exciting at first, but now I long for more serenity of spirit. I'm glad to be going home for a while."

It wasn't long before they turned left off the beach road and headed across a bridge over the river, toward the highway that would take them the rest of the way north. Lily thought she should stop soon to fill the tank, muttering about how few miles they would go on a gallon in this car. She pulled into a busy gas station just as, with a sudden *pfouuufff!*, Jack turned back into a lizard. He looked up at Lily. She saw the fear in his eyes and got out quickly, filled the tank, and guided the car back onto the road.

"I don't think anyone noticed," she said, as they drove away. "And I believe the Fairies are right and you will be returned to normal. I'm sure you're not the first human transformation Incantaro has had to reverse. Why don't you try to take a nap?" But Jack was not in the mood for that right now; his tail thumped the towel with agitation. "I know, I know," she said. "Let me sing you a song I learned when I was a little girl."

Lily began the lullaby in a sweet, clear voice. It told of Grandmother Moon and her love for her children on earth. The Moon promised that, even when she was out of sight, she was still nearby, and would soon return so that her beams would once again light up the dark night. The Fairies watched waves of blue and silver from her song surround Jack in a soft embrace. Soon the lizard's eyes closed and he was peaceful again. But Lily kept on singing for quite a while; probably, Melarose thought, to soothe herself. After all, it wasn't every day you returned home after a long absence in a big, black Hummer, with a lizard and two Fairies as companions.

Chapter 3

A WIZARD'S WARNING

A brilliant red-and-purple sunset stained the sky when the Hummer pulled into a rest stop. Melarose and Runawind had dozed off, too, and woke with a start when the car door slammed shut. Runawind fluttered to the window in time to see Lily disappear into the long, well-lit building. He looked over the top of the front seat and found that Jack was also awake. The lizard looked miserable, and Runawind thought he saw a tear fall from the eye that looked back at him. Runawind was touched; surprisingly so. He quietly fluttered back down to join Melarose between the suitcases.

Soon the car door opened and Lily reached in for her pack. She unzipped it and took out a small steel bowl, into which she poured some bottled water. She placed this, and some slices of apple, on the towel near Jack. He looked up at her and she looked away, saying, "I'm going to stretch my legs for a while." With that, she left the car again.

Melarose heard Jack approach the bowl, then the clumsy splash as he crawled partway in and began to drink. "How kind of Lily to let him have his privacy," Melarose thought.

Moments later, there was another splash as Jack left the water bowl, and not long after, Lily returned. She removed the bowl and dumped the water on some bushes nearby. Then she got back into the car, started the engine, and headed back onto the highway. They were now more than halfway through the ten-hour trip, and it seemed she meant to keep going until they got there. They heard her take a deep sigh.

"We can use some Fairy Dust to keep her clear and alert," Melarose whispered. Runawind nodded his agreement, and so they flew up to rest on Lily's shoulders.

"Are you doing okay back there?" Lily asked them.

"We're just fine, but we're going to sprinkle you with some Fairy Dust to make the rest of the drive easy," Runawind said.

"That's very kind, but won't you need it to give Jack more time as a human? I thought we might stop when it gets dark and no one can see into the car," Lily replied.

"Oh, we just need a tiny bit for you and, yes, we'll be able to give Jack a little more time, too," Runawind said.

He and Melarose fluttered above Lily's head, singing the ancient song of strength and clarity as they dropped a shimmering veil that landed in her hair and all along her shoulders. Lily's breath grew strong and deep.

"Ah. Thank you," she said. The last rays of sunlight pierced the sky. The whole journey now seemed blessed. "We'll be there soon," she crooned to Jack, who settled down comfortably at the sound of her voice.

Night fell. They passed the last major city on their route. Soon the road held less traffic and was lined by dense trees. Lily directed the car toward the shoulder. Melarose and Runawind took the hint—they quickly flew to the front seat and repeated the undoing spell, using all but the last tiny bit of Rainbow Fairy Dust. Once again, Jack returned to his human form.

When he looked at Lily now, his eyes were tender.

"Let's walk a little bit," Lily said, and they got out of the Hummer, with the Fairies following close behind. They were also anxious to feel the night air and move into the tree line for a while.

They were all greeted by a refreshing breeze. The clear, moonless sky was filled with stars. Jack was very happy to stretch his human legs. It was an odd thing for him to feel so peaceful; to be content walking on a dark roadside in silence with someone he hardly knew. He was more accustomed to the intensity of bright lights, noise, and the feeling of craving, seeking gratification, then craving again.

"How much longer?" he asked Lily, this time more to make conversation than from a need to know.

"A few hours. But it will be slow-going when we get onto the mountain itself," Lily answered, though she seemed far away in thought.

"Would you rather stop and rest for the night?" Jack asked, surprised again at his desire to consider her feelings. He could just make out her smile in the deepening night.

"Thank you, Jack," she said softly. "But I think we should go straight to the forest. The Fairies will help us with that part of the journey, and they have made sure that I am strong and my mind is clear."

"If you say so," he offered. "Lily," he began. "I've never known anyone like you. Will you tell me about yourself once we're back in the car and I am ..." he stopped himself from saying the words.

"Yes, I will," she promised reluctantly. They turned to head back. Not far from the car, they found Melarose laughing delightedly at Runawind, who was performing flying somersaults above a bush nearby.

"Time to go," Lily said.

Runawind stopped in mid-revolution and flashed a dazzling Fairy smile. "You're both so glum!" he cried. "We're on a great adventure. And soon you'll meet all the Fairy Folk and take part in a great miracle!" He fluttered up to Lily's shoulder. Despite his efforts, Lily only sighed. Jack said nothing at all.

The big doors to the Hummer clicked open and the Fairies flew in, finding their spot in the back. Jack fastened his seat belt, looked over at Lily, and seemed about to say something, when there was a sudden *pfoufff*! and he was once again a lizard, clutching the fibers of the towel to stop himself from falling off the seat headfirst.

Lily turned the key in the ignition, looked carefully back at the dark road behind them, and pulled onto the highway. Only when she had accelerated to the speed limit did she look over at Jack.

"Okay," she said. "I'm going to tell you about myself now." And, with that, she began a tale of a young girl, bored with small-town life in the North Carolina Mountains, who resisted her grandmother's desire to teach her more of the Native American ways. She already knew a few ceremonies, a few songs. It just hadn't seemed important to her to know more. She had bigger dreams, desires she had built from watching TV and reading magazines. On the eve of her eighteenth birthday, she thought her dream was coming true. She was working behind the register of a local convenience store when three young women she knew came in, looking for sodas and snacks.

"We're headed south," one of them bragged.

"So?" Lily had shrugged. To her, *south* meant the nearest town with a movie theater.

"No. We're going to Florida," another girl said. "For good. Jessie here got herself a job in a big beach resort, and we're going to get jobs too."

At this, Lily's eyes had flashed and her spirit turned. "Can I come?" she blurted out, before she could stop herself.

Calculating more help with the gas money, the second girl said, "Sure. But we're leaving in an hour ... just have to get our bags."

"I'll be ready ... meet me here!" Lily begged, although this meant closing the store early and abandoning her job and everyone, everything, she knew. She felt if she didn't take this chance, another would never come.

Melarose had fluttered up to Lily's shoulder. "What did your mother say?" she asked.

"I'll just have to imagine that," Lily said sadly. "I didn't want anyone to interfere, so I snuck into the house, grabbed my things, ran back, and waited behind the store. Part of me didn't think they'd come back for me at all. But they did."

"And then what happened?" Melarose was all ears.

"I got a job at the resort, taking care of the plants and tropical birds. For a while, it was bliss ... going out to clubs at night, meeting exciting people from all over the world." She sighed again. "But, one day, the excitement faded. The people seemed shallow and sometimes cruel. One of my friends landed in the hospital from taking too many drugs." She paused. "I stopped going to the clubs, bought some tobacco and sage, and did some prayers in the old way. Shortly after, I met the people with the big house on the beach and they asked me if I'd like to move into their guest cottage to watch the house for them and care for their birds. I was ready for some quiet time, so I said yes. That was five years ago."

"So, now you're ashamed and afraid of how people will treat you when you get back home?" Runawind inquired bluntly, from the top of the passenger seat.

"Wouldn't you be?" Lily asked.

"Wouldn't *we* be?!" Melarose and Runawind echoed back at her. "Why, no," Melarose continued. "Those who love us always seek to understand. They don't punish us if we make a mistake, but they're happy to see us find the right way again." She looked at Runawind, who beamed at her. "I'm sure you'll find the same is true for you."

"I hope you're right," Lily replied. "I did write to them over the years, and I called a few times; but I never went back. It isn't very far from Grandfather Mountain … a few hours to the west. I hope Jack will drive me over there once he is in human form again."

"Oh!" Melarose exclaimed. "Jack would do anything for you, I'm sure! After all, you have done so much for him by bringing him to the Great Forest. How else would we have gotten back?"

Runawind saw the lizard look away. He wondered if Melarose was right. Once Jack was back in control, things could look a lot different to him than they did now. He remembered Lily's words in the garden. Would Jack have enough strength of character to become a human being once he was in the form of a man again?

It was close to midnight when the big Hummer came to the end of the dirt road that led deep into the Great Forest. Jack spent the last few miles of bumping along clinging for dear life to the towel on the passenger seat, while the Fairies flitted up and down on the tops of the suitcases. Thanks to the Fairy Dust, Lily was fine. She parked the car in a small clearing, took some things out of the top of her backpack, and told Jack to get inside. Reluctantly, he did. Melarose and Runawind were so excited to arrive home that they began to glow. This would be helpful, too, as they would have to guide Lily into the woods with only dim starlight to make the rough trail visible.

High up on Grandfather Mountain, the night air was cool. Lily got into the back of the Hummer and unzipped her suitcase. She quickly changed into sweatpants, sweater, and sweatshirt, and traded her sandals for socks and tennis shoes. Opening the front passenger door, she put the pack on her back, took her flashlight from the passenger seat, shut the door, and stood waiting. If she hadn't grown up in mountains just like this one, she might have been afraid, but she seemed calm and ready.

"This way!" Runawind cried, and they all set off on the thin dirt trail that began at the edge of the road.

Their trip into the Great Forest had barely begun, when the trees next to them suddenly filled with small incandescent lights of white and blue. Some moved slowly through the branches and others hovered in place. "We're back!" Melarose cried, unable to contain her joy at being home again. "We're back—and we have some new friends with us, too!"

In a blink, the lights became a happy, cheering crowd of Fairy Folk, who rushed forward to meet Runawind and Melarose, and inspect this human who walked with them. Lily smiled as many of them flew right up to her face, peering into her eyes. She felt some brush her shoulders and she knew they hoped to get a peek into the backpack that had begun to bulge in odd places as the lizard became agitated.

"This is Lily White Dove," Runawind said. "Lily, meet our family ... well, part of it!"

"I am enchanted," Lily offered, and the Fairies fluttered happily among small bubbles of pink and gold light that moved on the wave of her delighted laughter. "Or, more truthfully, I am very happy to see you all. It's my friend in the backpack who is truly enchanted." Another generous peal of laughter sent more bubbles waving around them.

"Yes," Melarose hurried to explain. "We must meet with Incantaro and the Circle of Seven to hear what can be done. Jack was turned into a lizard on Midsummer's Eve— we must see if he can become a human again!"

The Greatest Enchantment

And, so, off they all went, one group of Fairies flying close to Runawind, another with Melarose, soaking up the feeling of their adventure. Every now and then, a Fairy would leave the group and approach the backpack, then realize that even an enchanted lizard must have a long tongue, decide not to investigate further, and flutter back to join the others.

In a short while, they found themselves in the clearing, and approached the great ring of mushrooms. Melarose and Runawind led Lily to the center. The other Fairies formed a ring within the ring and began to call out, "Incantaro and the Circle of Seven! Approach us now, please! We have need of you!"

A brilliant flash of white, gold, and electric blue in front of Lily announced the arrival of Incantaro and the rest of the Fairy wizards. Lily pressed her right hand to her heart and bowed her head in a gesture of loving respect.

"What have we here?" Incantaro peered happily at the lovely Lily and her squirming backpack. Lily placed the pack on the floor and lifted the lizard out, holding it before her. Runawind and Melarose hovered on either side of Lily, waiting for her to speak.

"Great Wizard Elders of the Fairy Folk, this lizard is my friend Jack. He has been enchanted, and we wish to free him now, if you see fit."

"And why was the spell cast?" Incantaro came closer to look into Jack's lizard eyes. Jack pulled his head back and tried to turn away. But, everywhere he turned, there was another wizard fluttering near him, peering into his eyes. If a lizard could sweat, Jack would be sweating now.

When Lily seemed at a loss for words, Runawind spoke up. "We met some Fairy Folk in The Land That Has No Fall. And they were pretty strange, let me tell you!" Runawind started to lose himself in laughter, but the stern look from Incantaro brought him back to the subject. "They believed that Jack was hurting the people of the land by destroying the habitats of all kingdoms and building large houses that only the rich could own. The weather was changed as he and others dried up the wetlands for their own gain, and then machines flew in the sky, spreading deadly sprays to kill off the biting insects. But those sprays killed all things in their path, even an unfortunate Fairy. On Midsummer's Eve, those Fairies felt that Jack deserved to be seen in his true light, and so they turned him into a lizard."

"I see," Incantaro murmured, stroking his beard and carefully observing Jack's agitated state. "And how did you come to help him?"

Runawind broke into uncontrolled giggles at the thought of Arnold. Melarose shot him a sidelong glance and began, "When I was seeking proper shelter, we met Arnold, one of the Fairies from that place. Jack captured him and threatened to kill him unless we helped him break the enchantment and become a man again."

"And you?" Incantaro asked Lily, approaching her face now and gazing into her eyes. "You were not captured, too? Oh, yes, yes. I see how it is. In a way, you were. And now you want to trust him and help him heal." Lily closed her eyes, to hold back tears. "You will please wait here with your friend," the Wizard said. "I will deliberate with my Council." And, with that, Incantaro and the Circle of Seven vanished in a bright burst of white.

"What should I do?" Lily asked Melarose, who had sat on her shoulder for support. "What if they won't grant the reversal?"

"Don't worry, we'll know soon, and then ..." Melarose began, but before she could finish, there was another flash of white and the wizards were back. Melarose could feel Lily trembling.

"The matter is complicated," Incantaro began. "There is nothing to suggest Jack's innocence. Even his behavior with Arnold shows that he thinks of himself before all others. And it seems the Fairies' assessment of his true nature is not without merit." Lily sighed, hearing this truth she herself had expressed. "But we have come to a decision that will help everyone and still teach Jack the error of his ways," Incantaro said. The Fairies, Lily, and the lizard leaned forward to hear what this might be.

"Listen well, Lizard," Incantaro decreed, in his most solemn voice. "You will be restored to your human body this night. But there is more."

The Greatest Enchantment

"More!" cried the Circle of Seven. "Mark it well, Lizard, for you have no other way!"

"Whenever you fall into a thought that is harmful to another, whenever you choose to go back to your old, selfish ways, a three-inch square of scales will appear in place of your own flesh. It will begin with your feet, which show the way you walk in this world," Incantaro said. Noting Jack's relief, and reading his thoughts, he continued, "And, no, it will not be possible to remove them; not even by cutting them away. No matter what you do, they will grow back."

"And if his whole body becomes covered with scales?" Lily asked calmly, acknowledging the wisdom in this decision.

"When the patch that takes up more than half of his body forms, he will turn into a lizard again. Then, no charm, no ritual performed by any kind of wizard anywhere, will be able to lift the change, and his transformation will be complete." Incantaro turned to Jack. "So, you see, it will be, as it always was, up to you to choose your true nature."

Incantaro started to fly back to the Council group, but instead, turned to face Jack again. "We grant you another kindness as an opportunity for growth. You will go with Lily to her family and spend a full moon-cycle before you may return to your home. You must be with someone who is kind and who loves you now." Incantaro saw Lily's blush and gave her his sweetest smile. "In that healing company, you might become a true human being. It is your best chance for success."

"But how will he be made to stay?" Lily asked. "If he wants to leave, I mean."

"The scales will begin to form. He'll quickly see that there is no way he can assert his will over the will of the Council," Incantaro laughed merrily, as he flew back to join the Circle of Seven. They hovered together a moment and, at a signal from Incantaro, began a sacred chant.

"Put Jack down," Runawind advised, and Lily placed the oddly quiet, compliant lizard on the grass next to her.

The chanting of the Council filled the ring with a glowing golden light. Lily began to have lovely visions of the white doves that would play near her when she was a child. She remembered the gentle way she approached them, and how soon they would be cooing, taking breadcrumbs from her hand. Lost in this happy memory, she had no idea how long the chanting had gone on, when suddenly it ceased and she once again saw the ring and the Fairies, and next to her stood Jack. His eyes were closed and he was smiling, as if he were seeing a happy vision, too. He seemed more peaceful than she had ever known him to be.

Incantaro came forward from the Council group and placed a tiny pouch in Lily's hand.

"If you ever need me, I will come to you." And after Lily thanked him and put the pouch in her pocket, he turned to Jack. "Wake...wake...w*ake*!" he commanded, and Jack opened his eyes. "You remember all that was told to you as a lizard? You know the will of the Council, and what you must do now?"

"Yes," Jack said. "I remember it all." He turned to Lily and smiled.

"Should we be going now, Incantaro?" Lily asked.

"Oh no! It's far too late, and you are both tired," Incantaro said, and laughed his merry laugh. "The Fairies have been busy creating a resting place for you. When the birds begin their song to greet the sun, you will rise, refreshed and ready for what lies ahead." He gestured to Melarose and Runawind. "You may show them to their beds and then join us all in our celebration of your homecoming ... which, though shorter than most, still demands that all must be told before the sunrise."

"Short?" Runawind asked, with unhappy surprise.

"Oh, you two will go with Jack and Lily, didn't I say?" Incantaro teased. "These mortals have great need of your friendship to help them at this time. And of course you would be so curious to know how they are doing, would you not?" There was a flash of gold light, and Incantaro was gone.

Runawind and Melarose looked at each other, then at Jack and Lily. They beckoned the mortals to follow them to the bower that the other Fairies had prepared. Once there, a last sprinkle of Fairy Dream Powder put the two mortals quickly into a deep sleep. Melarose sighed her prettiest sigh; then turned to smile at Runawind.

"It's okay. Incantaro's right," she said, hovering close to him and planting a Fairy kiss on his nose. Runawind blushed to his toes. "Just think! Ours is a tale that's sure to be told forever at the Great Festival," she said. "And our next trip is not so far from home. We'll be back before the leaves turn gold."

"I like the way that sounds ... 'our' next trip." Runawind began a flying somersault, but stopped midway. "But when the forest changes ...?" he began.

"When the leaves turn orange, gold, and red; drift from the trees; and cover the ground in a soft, bright carpet?" She enjoyed watching Runawind hang on her words. "Then I will love this time as I have loved no other!" she concluded.

Runawind beamed his relief and completed his somersault, adding another for good measure. Melarose laughed her loveliest silvery Fairy laugh and, holding hands, they joyously flew off to tell the others their tale of The Land That Has No Fall.

Chapter 4

HOME AGAIN

Lily woke as the rising sun's rays filtered through the trees. She sat up, remembered where she was, and what had happened the night before. She thought of how—just like that night years ago in Cherokee—her life had unexpectedly changed again; it was now on a completely different course. And again, she had no idea where it would take her. Lily looked over at the mossy bed where Jack still lay sleeping, and sighed. This was his chance—hers, too. He might learn to develop a new way of thinking and remain in his human body. She might reconcile with her family and find peace. But things could still go terribly wrong for both of them. She lay back down and looked up at the stars, fading in the lightening sky.

"Lily." The soft whisper stopped her anxious thoughts. "Lily?" Lowering her gaze, she saw Melarose and Runawind fluttering close-by. Putting a finger to her lips, she gestured toward Jack.

"But Lily," Runawind said. "You must both get ready to leave."

"I know," she agreed, then sighed again. "I'll go and say my prayers. Please wake Jack when I'm gone." She rose slowly and looked around for a pathway to follow.

Melarose flew off to accompany her. She knew Lily would need a lot of support today.

When they were both out of sight, Runawind fluttered next to Jack's left ear. "Jack," he said. There was no response.

"Jack?" he tried again. There was still no response, so he took a deep breath and bellowed, "Jack!" But it seemed that Jack had not heard him. He wondered if maybe the sleeping charm had been too strong in Jack's case. Or maybe now that Jack was free of his lizard enchantment and was a man again, he couldn't hear the Fairies.

When Lily and Melarose came back, they saw Runawind on Jack's chest, riding the rise and fall of his deep-sleep breath.

"What's the matter?" Lily asked.

"He doesn't hear me," Runawind said. "You wake him—then we'll know if he can see us."

Lily pondered this. "It's probably best if he doesn't," she said and smiled. "What's happened will confuse him enough. He should remember the curse being lifted and Incantaro's words of warning. But I think he'll behave more freely and be true to his real nature if he thinks other humans are the only ones who can see or hear him."

"We'll do a thought charm for the three of us," Melarose suggested. "Then we can communicate when we aren't alone."

"A wonderful idea," Runawind agreed, beaming at her. They set about opening the gates for clear telepathy, and when they were satisfied all was working well, Lily bent down to wake Jack. With a mother's tender touch, she caressed his hair. Her sweet voice sent pink waves toward the ear of the sleeping man.

With a great snort, Jack shook himself awake and sat up, looking all around. "Oh," he groaned. "It wasn't a dream after all."

"No. Not a dream," Lily said. "We must get ready and leave the forest now. Do you remember what the wizard told you last night?"

"I think so," he muttered, getting up and brushing moss off his shirt. Runawind was flying circles around Jack's head, but Jack gave no sign that he noticed.

"I'll remind you on the drive. Remember where we're going, and why?"

"You can remind me of that, too. The only thing on my mind right now is food. I feel like I haven't eaten in weeks," he said. "And that's probably true."

"We'll stop at the diner we passed last night," she said, thinking a steaming cup of coffee would do them both a lot of good.

Two hours later, Jack pushed back what was left of his second plate of pancakes and bacon, gulped down the last of his fifth cup of coffee, and said he was ready to go.

"Is there any place we can pick up some clothes on the way?" he asked. He'd had plenty of time to observe the other diners and realized his Florida style was not going to fit in here. And his silk shirt definitely hadn't given him enough protection from the surprisingly cool morning air on Grandfather Mountain.

"Sure. We'll pass an outlet mall near Asheville on the way," Lily replied. She'd been pushing what was left of her food around the plate while he ate, her growing anxiety about their destination making it hard for her to eat very much. Any excuse to stop on the way was welcome. "About the car…" she began.

"I thought of that, too," Jack said. When they'd pulled into the diner's parking lot, a quick glance around told him his car was calling attention to them; but not the kind he wanted.

"It will take lots of gas to get up into the mountains," she said. "And if we go off-road, there are branches that would mark up the sides." This was true … but she really didn't want to show up at her Momma's house in the Hummer. A display of wealth and waste was not the way to cross the bridge with her family.

"I'll find a rental and leave the Hummer with them till we get back," he offered.

That settled, Jack paid the bill, and they set off again. Lily was in the driver's seat since she knew the way. Runawind and Melarose peered out the windows from the top of the back seat, where they'd opted to stay, taking in as much green energy as they could from the scenery.

They stopped first at the outlet mall where they could find all they'd need for mountain life. Lily found shopping with Jack surprisingly exciting. He didn't even look at price tags; just piled things he liked for them both into a cart and pushed it toward the dressing rooms. He asked her to model for him, indicating his approval, or wrinkling his nose. She discovered she was expected to listen to him, over her own likes and dislikes.

She came out now in something she had picked out—a large, loose-fitting, red cable knit sweater that would be perfect for layering over a shirt and jeans. This got a wrinkled nose from Jack. Lily glanced at Melarose, hovering nearby, to get the encouragement she needed.

"I know you don't like it," she told Jack. "But I'll be warm and comfortable in this when it gets a lot cooler. I'd really like to have it."

After a slight pause, Jack agreed. Lily glowed, feeling more optimistic about his chances of succeeding in his mission. But Runawind saw Jack's sly, sideways glance at this, and again, as Lily smiled at his approval when she came out in something he'd picked — black leggings, and a fitted beige suede shirt with fringe. Runawind wondered if a small plaque of lizard scales had just formed on Jack's foot. He knew Jack could, and would, use Lily's desire to be accepted; but he wasn't yet sure of the purpose. And he also saw that several shopping bags full of clothes and a new pair of tooled, red leather boots could be working their own magic on Lily, too.

"Okay. Which car?" Jack asked later, when they pulled into the Rental Car lot. "Pick something comfortable, but not flashy."

Lily scanned the waiting cars and pointed to a dark blue, midsize SUV.

"Okay," Jack said. "How long will we need it?"

"About a month," she said. Aware he wasn't happy to hear this, she quickly added, "That's what Incantaro suggested. But they'll let you return it sooner, won't they?"

He grinned, but his eyes weren't smiling. "Wait here," he said.

She watched him stride into the office and turned to the Faeries. "Well, what do you think?" Melarose fluttered up to the front seat. "You might need to talk to him about what Incantaro and the Circle of Seven decided last night. I think he could use a gentle reminder," she said.

"I'll say he does," Runawind exclaimed, flying up front to join her. "Lily, please be careful. Jack can be charming; you told us so yourself. But I think there may be a couple of lizard scale patches on his foot already."

Lily sighed. "I know. You're right. This isn't going to be easy."

"That's true," Melarose agreed. "But don't give up. Just try to see clearly. Being fooled by him won't help either of you."

"I'm so glad you two are here to remind me. And you'll see that Jack won't be able to charm all of my family. I'm sure I'll get a talking to from one of them if I seem headed for danger."

Runawind thought about how she had described her family to Jack while they drove. There was her mother, Rose, and her younger brother, Billy. There were too many uncles, aunts, and cousins to remember all their names. Her voice trembled when she said her father died years ago, and it dropped to a whisper when she mentioned her Grandmother, Sarah Rainmaker. Jack looked out at the mountains the whole time. He was listening, though, and asked some general questions about each person, but Runawind knew it wasn't for Lily's sake. Jack wanted information he could use as a way to ingratiate himself.

"Do you feel ready to see them now?" Runawind asked.

"Not really. I think I'd better call Momma where she works. Surprising them is not a great idea." She took out the Smart Phone Jack had insisted on getting her when they were at the shopping mall. "I hope Momma understands. I hope they will all forgive me for disappearing the way I did," Lily said, staring at her short contacts list.

"Humans seem to be full of hope," Runawind said.

"Don't Fairies hope?"

"Yes. But it's a little different," he replied.

"This is a question for Incantaro," Melarose interjected.

"If you really want to know, he'll tell you," Runawind agreed.

"I would really like to know," Lily said. "But we're far from Grandfather Mountain now."

"A question this important deserves my instant reply." Incantaro's voice suddenly filled the car. He chuckled at her surprise. "For you must understand that hope filled with enthusiasm that expects the best outcome is far different than hope born of fear and worry. Fairies hope with enthusiasm, while humans often hope with fear." Incantaro paused. "Runawind

The Greatest Enchantment

hoped to find a place where Melarose would never be sad again, and despite his reservations about the trip itself, he set off, confident that they would find what they were looking for. As you now know, it didn't turn out the way they had both imagined. But they found something far greater than their own ideas had been. It brought them to you, and to each other. And Melarose was also released from a slight misperception." He chuckled again. "You had hoped to overcome your guilt about leaving your family. You had hoped that Jack might notice you. The fear in these hopes simply holds you back from seeing and accepting the perfection of what is brought to you. You miss the gifts in each moment by looking too far ahead for a specific outcome that you don't even believe will happen. Do you understand?" he concluded.

"Yes. I think I do," Lily replied.

"Then know this, too—when a group of people hopes with fear, it leaves them open to despair and defeat. They can turn their back on life if they don't see what they believe is the right outcome. This is difficult for humans to realize," he said. "And group agreement makes it even harder. It is necessary for each individual to come to their own understanding of hope. Then they must live it. The more that do, the more the group will shift as a whole. These principles have been demonstrated time and again, but are rarely heeded." He paused. "Remember this, Lily White Dove, and with confident enthusiasm, hope to put it to good use," he said. His voice was a far off whisper as he added, "Remember, Lily White Dove, you can call on me."

After a few silent moments, Lily let out a big exhale and said, "I guess he really meant that promise to me."

"Why wouldn't he?" Melarose asked. Since it was not the Fairy way to make and break promises, she couldn't understand why Lily thought Incantaro would fail her.

"Right," Lily said. "I think I just learned another difference between your world and ours. The Fairy realm seems a much better place than mine."

"Humans have thought that before. Some sought us out, accepted our offers of food and drink, and danced with us in the Fairy Ring, wishing to stay," Runawind said. "Some even married Elves and had offspring. But eventually, most come to miss the humans they left behind and are sad when it is impossible to find their way back to them. Our time is not like yours, you see. There are not too many portals between our realms; those time junctures are necessary to completely enter or leave the Fairy Realm. And even if they did manage to get back, they could find themselves in quite a different time than the one they left."

"But you're here with me now. And so were the other Fairies last night," Lily wondered.

"It's our gift to pass between the worlds," Melarose said. "The Elemental Fairies, Sylphs, Naiads, Elves, and Salamanders—even the largest of the Trolls can pass through worlds this way and experience the different timelines. Lily, do you ever wonder why you and just a few other adult humans can see and hear us?"

"Grandma Sarah can see Fairies, too," Lily remembered. "I did ask her once why Momma and Daddy thought I was making it up. She just laughed and gave me a cupcake with chocolate icing. I guess that was enough to end my questioning. I just didn't bother to tell anyone again."

"Maybe she'll explain if you ask her now," Runawind said.

"Maybe," Lily said. She took a few deep breaths. "I hope with happy expectation that Momma will answer the phone, and that she'll be glad to hear it's me, and that I'm on my way home." She called the tourist shop in town where Momma worked.

Her mother answered, but Melarose could see tears forming in Lily's eyes and knew Lily was having a hard time accepting the gift in what she was hearing. The short conversation was over with Lily's soft, 'Goodbye.'

"She says her house is full and I should call Uncle Will. Or we can get a hotel room," Lily reported. The tears began to fall. "But she did say she was glad. And she's sure my Grandmother will want to see me soon."

"What will you do?" Melarose asked.

"I'll ask Jack. He'll probably want to stay at a hotel anyway. But I would like to call Uncle Will," she said, regaining her composure. "He has a big house, near the top of a mountain. I remember seeing the sunsets from his porch." She sighed. "He's been all alone there since Aunt Josie died, and their sons moved east."

"Jack's coming," Runawind warned.

Lily dried her cheeks and lowered the car window to get her instructions.

Not long after, she pulled the rented SUV into a parking space in a multi-story indoor garage. Jack had said he wanted to walk around downtown Asheville before choosing a restaurant for lunch. "The streets and buildings remind me of older towns up north," he said, as they drove into the main street of this artsy mountain town. Lily had never been north, so she had to believe this was true. "And that's more like New York City," he said, pointing to some young people in baggy clothes—arms covered in colorful tattoos and sporting streaks of red, purple or blue in their hair—who were congregating on a busy corner. "New Age hippies," he laughed. It was the first time on their trip that she had seen him delighted. And so she was happy to stop in Asheville, and had quickly found a place where they wouldn't have to worry about fearing time on the meter.

She sent a thought to the Fairies as she left the car. "You'll be safe here, but there won't be much to see."

"We could both use some sleep." Runawind sent this reply along with a giggle. But as they watched Jack and Lily go, a strange thing happened that made sleep unlikely.

Two young men were heading in the direction of the SUV. Their gait wavered, they appeared spacey and depressed, and they were not alone. The Fairies gasped, wide-eyed, at the Shadows floating alongside the unsuspecting humans. '*Specters*,' as they were sometimes called, these tall gray shadows haunted the Otherworld, too. No spirits of the elemental realm welcomed the sight of them. Only a few were brave enough to challenge a Shadow and make it disappear because, without the utmost care and strength of purpose, before being able to overpower it, a Shadow could quietly attach and begin to feed on the energy of whatever it came upon. When that happened, an overwhelming feeling of gloom quickly quenched the fires of individuality. Eventually, the host for the Shadow became its unwitting servant. While this was more likely to happen to a being whose will was already low, it wasn't wise to take a chance. Despite being strong of will and purpose, the Fairies were weakened now by having been so long in an unnatural environment.

"Down here," Runawind pointed to a gap between two tall shopping bags. They fluttered down the paper tunnel to the car's carpeted floor. They would remain here; silent, still, and suspending all thought, to mask their presence for any other Shadow that might be lurking nearby.

It might have been mere minutes, or endless hours, till two short beeps unlocked the doors of the SUV, and they were startled back to the present. As the doors opened, they heard Jack telling Lily how much fun Asheville had been.

Lily sent them a worried thought asking where they might be. They used telepathy to let her know what had happened. Lily frowned.

"What's wrong?" Jack asked as Lily started the car.

"Nothing, just feeling a little worried about seeing Momma," she replied.

"Oh. Well, you'll be fine," he said and quickly continued on about Asheville's great food and interesting shops. "This would be a terrific place to put some money into a downtown renovation project," he concluded.

"Jack," Lily said. "Do you hear what you're saying? Don't you see what would happen if these interesting old buildings are torn down and replaced by tall modern ones?"

"Yes," Jack said, amused by her concern. "People in the high floor offices and apartments would have stunning views of the mountains."

Lily groaned. "But no one else would. The streets would be darkened from lack of sunlight. And what about all those charming shops you loved? Could they afford the higher rents? This town would be ruined, Jack. That's what would happen."

It was Jack's turn to groan—partly from what Lily was saying, but also from feeling another patch of lizard skin form on his right ankle. He knew he had gained a few of them since this morning and was not looking forward to seeing what would be there when he took his socks off later.

"You didn't believe Incantaro, did you?" Lily asked. There was no reply, and Jack was silent for most of the drive to Cherokee.

This gave Lily a lot of time to think about her own situation. The thought of calling Uncle Will seemed to have a glow around it and created a warm feeling of comfort. She would definitely get his number from Momma and call as soon as she was in her hotel room. The thought of seeing Grandma Rainmaker felt like a force of reckoning. She thought that this must be where she would truly be making her amends.

When they were getting closer to Cherokee, Runawind fluttered up to land on her left shoulder. "Don't answer," he said out loud, knowing Jack couldn't hear him. "But is there somewhere we can stop soon; somewhere Melarose and I can have time out among the trees? Being inside buildings and cars for so long has made us feel weak."

Lily thought for a moment. "Jack," she said. "There's a beautiful waterfall just up the road. I'd like to stop and say some prayers there, if you don't mind."

"Sure," he said, still glum. "Better say some for me, too, please." He was so sincere that it touched her heart.

"I hope you'll come to the falls with me," she said softly. "It's very beautiful and the energy will recharge you, too."

He gave her a quizzical look, but she knew he would give it a try.

And she knew this place was very special. Every one of the many waterfalls she had been to in this area had its own special nature. Some were gentle and evoked reminiscence; others were active and inspiring; some seemed to sing of the old times and invoke Spirits; others expanded the heart with love, creating joy. The one they were going to now was like a wise old grandfather who spoke in a deep, reassuring voice. It helped a person find answers within. It was the perfect place for them to visit before coming into town.

They drove into the parking lot, and found that, since it was later on a weekday at summer's end, only a few others were also visiting this spot. With luck, Lily thought, we'll be alone when we get to the falls.

"We'll take care of that," Runawind said. Melarose giggled.

Getting out of the car, Lily watched the Fairies fly quickly past her and disappear into the dense woods lining the trail. She could feel how happy and relieved they were to be back in nature. And so was she.

Jack closed the passenger door and walked around to where she stood. She smiled, giving him a pinch of loose tobacco, and led the way to the trail head. Here, she stopped, and told Jack to copy her motions. She took her own pinch of tobacco, holding it up first to the sky, then to the earth, her heart, and her lips; saying 'thank you,' as she released the tobacco onto the ground.

"This place is home to many creatures, and we are their guests," she explained. "We show respect when we honor them before we enter. Now they know we come in peace and goodwill."

It would not be a difficult hike, but she was glad they had replaced their sandals with new shoes that were perfect for walking in any situation. Fortunately, the trail was clear and dry. The air was moist and noticeably cooler. All weariness from being on the road began to melt away, and the steady gurgle of the creek running alongside made her spirits rise.

They passed two families and a couple who were wandering back out with bemused looks on their faces. Lily was grateful to find that she and Jack were, indeed, alone when they came upon the full view of the falls. Melarose and Runawind were already there, happily dipping and soaring, along with several bright-yellow butterflies, through the thin mist that rose from the long column of cascading water. Afternoon sunlight streamed through the tall pines, creating diamond sparkles where white water hit small boulders at the base of the falls.

Lily filled her lungs with the invigorating air. "Isn't he beautiful?" she asked.

"He?"

"Close your eyes, breathe and feel," she said. "When you feel that the sound of the falls is holding you as your grandfather did when you were little, think of a question that your heart needs answered. Wait quietly to hear. This old Grandfather will always answer the questions of your heart."

Lily was happy to see Jack quietly do as he was told. She moved a little further off and began her prayers. Holding another pinch of tobacco, she began a traditional song, to honor and recognize the spirits of this place; then she sang her request for an audience with her spirit guides and the Grandfather of the waterfall. When she finished, she released the tobacco into the water and thought about her own heart questions. Of course, she had more than one, and she didn't expect to hear the replies all at once. But because she knew she would receive guidance in time, she finished with a 'thank you' song to release her spirit guides and indicate gratitude. Grandma Rainmaker had taught her to always say 'thank you,' even before receiving the things she desired; saying this showed confidence in the goodness of Spirit, and empowered manifestation.

She looked over at Jack. Tears glistened on his cheeks. She went to him and took him in her arms. He began to sob, releasing the tension of his recent experiences. Melarose and Runawind heard and quickly flew over. Lily smiled at their surprised expressions and sent them a thought, "It seems he is partly human, after all." Melarose planted a soft Fairy Kiss on Jack's brow, and followed Runawind, who was already heading back to continue the very interesting conversation they had been having with the Guardian of the waterfall.

The majestic old Snake had scales in several shades of gray that allowed her to blend well with the rock on which she was coiled. A light stripe ran along the center of her back, charcoal stripes were on either side, and the lighter gray resumed on her belly. A forked black tongue flashed in and out of her mouth while she spoke. She had already told the Fairies that this was a sacred area to the People who had lived here, long before the Cherokee arrived. These falls, and their Guardian, had seen the more recent humans slowly change their ways, until most had lost their ability to know and connect with all that lived around them.

"Yesssssssssss," the Snake hissed at them when they returned. "Many will release sorrow in the lap of the Grandfather. To lose the natural connection to creation can only bring pain and suffering. But humans are proud. They ignore this feeling of unease and believe they control all they see." Her head rose up as she laughed at this, moving up and down and side to side. Recovering her dignity, she said, "Even though he is no longer honored, this Grandfather still exerts his influence. He does so for the wise and the lost, in equal measure. Sssssssstill," she hissed, "Why does this man who emits scarlet rays cry on the lovely woman's shoulder?"

Runawind told a bit of the story, including what Jack had gone through. "Of course, being a lizard is not at all like being a Snake," he quickly added.

Turning her head, the Snake considered him with a penetrating look from one bright black eye. "Yesssssssss. You are quite right. An elemental, like yourself, would know this well. There are not many in the human world as wise as you; not many humans still view us with respect, and honor us for our powers and medicine. They recoil from us in horror, as if the only thought we have is harm. I must endure the jagged energy of their shrieks when they manage to catch a glimpse of me, though I am far off and pose them no threat. It's a wonder that my sense of patience is not completely gone." She raised her regal head high, moving it slightly back and forth. "But I am here because Grandfather requires me."

"Of course," Melarose added. "As all sacred water places require their beloved Snake Guardians. You provide a great service for all the water creatures here, too—like those," she cried in delight, spotting a small group of naiads swimming in the creek. Their infectious peals of laughter made her giggle.

"Yessssssssss," the Snake hissed, commanding attention once again. "But the sun is getting low. I must get back to my home." She began to uncoil her long body and move slowly away. "I wish you well."

"Goodbye. Thank you for your story," the Fairies called after her, as she silently disappeared behind the tall boulder. "I guess we should get back to Lily," Ruanwind said. Off they flew.

They arrived in time to see Jack straighten back up, looking embarrassed. He drew his shirt sleeve over his cheeks to remove any trace of his tears. "I'm sorry," he said. "I've never done that before."

"Don't be sorry—please. You've probably never been a lizard before, or had to experience this kind of ordeal," she tried to joke, which didn't seem to work. "I'm glad you were able to release some of it now."

"Well," he said, a bit more gruffly. "I guess we should get going if we want to make it to Cherokee in time."

"In time for what?" she asked.

"To see your mother—where she works."

"Oh. Yes. That's probably a good idea," she said, grateful and surprised that he had thought of this. Was Grandfather answering one of her questions now?

"Give it time, Lily" Runawind cautioned.

"But stay hopeful," Melarose added.

"Okay," Lily said, to all of them. "Let's go."

Lily's Mom was busy with customers when they entered the brightly lit, wood-paneled souvenir shop. She seemed more fragile than Lily remembered; but still slim, with short black hair and bright red lipstick. Jack began to look around, attracted by a display of silver belt buckles.

Lily walked over to her mother's counter and waited. She was rewarded with a smile, although her mother continued to focus her attention on two women who were trying to decide which of the dangling turquoise earrings would look best on their niece. Once the transaction was done, her mother beckoned for her to come behind the counter, and gave her a hurried hug.

"I wasn't sure I'd ever see you again," Momma Rose said.

"I know. I'm sorry," Lily replied, tears forming and threatening to overflow.

"I understood better than you know, Lily," her mother said. "I almost left here myself. In those days, it was different for us than it is now."

Lily knew her mother referred to the way people thought about Indians back when Momma was her age. There was much more respect for what people now called 'Native Americans' than there had been; more interest in their ways. When her mother was a child, they were still thought of as 'savages'—pictured as tomahawk-wielding 'bad guys' in the many popular western films and television shows. Lily was grateful that most people she met reacted well when they heard her heritage.

"Then, I had you," her mother said. Was that regret Lily heard?

"Momma," Lily said. "I'm glad to be back here in the mountains. You might be, too, if you could see what's happening to many other places now."

"Maybe," Momma said, turning her attention to putting the more expensive earrings back in the locked case.

"Can I pay for this here?" The question startled both women out of their separate reveries.

"Momma, this is my friend, Jack Lerner... my mother, Rose Bryant." Lily said. Her mother kept her eyes on Jack's the whole time.

"I'm pleased to meet you. May I call you Rose?" Jack said.

"Yes, of course," she answered, accepting Jack's offered hand. "Thanks for bringing my little girl home."

"You're welcome, but it's Lily who brought me here." Jack was pouring on the charm and Lily watched for signs in her mother's expression. She knew 'little girl' had been a veiled warning. "I look forward to seeing more of this beautiful area and meeting the rest of her family."

Momma couldn't hold back a laugh. "That will take quite a while," she said. "There's a lot of us. Are you staying long?"

Jack gave her a big smile. "We'll see," he said. "I guess a lot depends on your little girl, here."

Jack can certainly return a serve, Lily thought. The game was clearly on.

"Momma," Lily interjected. "I want to find a hotel and get settled before dinner. Can you meet us later?"

"Not tonight," Momma said. "It's Wednesday." This was followed by a meaningful pause. On Wednesday evenings, people were back at Church for midweek service and an early supper. Lily had completely forgotten that aspect of life.

"Of course, Momma," she apologized. "We've been on the road and I completely forgot what day it was."

"Tomorrow," Momma said.

"Wonderful," Jack replied. "Bring Billy, and anyone else. You'll be my guests at any restaurant you choose."

Momma couldn't help but brighten at that. She gave Lily another quick hug and shooed her back around the counter. "Call me tomorrow," she told her—and to Jack, "Yes, I can ring that up for you here."

"Well, that wasn't so bad, was it?" Jack asked when they got into the car.

"Better than I expected," Lily admitted.

"I've already got rooms booked for two nights at the Casino hotel," Jack said. She wasn't surprised to hear he'd chosen one of the most expensive places to stay. "I booked them just before I came over with that buckle," he continued. "They have a Spa, so I also reserved massage appointments for us both before dinner. I definitely need one."

Lily had never had this kind of luxury before, but her body told her to accept the offer. "Thank you," she said. "I'm sure it will help me, too. But there's one place I'd like to see before we go on to the hotel. It won't take long, and it's on the way."

Jack agreed, so Lily drove out of town, and turned onto a road that led up a mountain. Only a few older homes were visible from the road. "You can go on up to Uncle Will's house. It's near the top," she thought for Runawind and Melarose. "I know you'll be happier there than in a hotel room."

"Thank you, Lily," Melarose said. "I think we've had our fill of cars and buildings."

"Yes," Runawind said. "I can't wait to investigate this area." As if to prove it, he fluttered up and down in front of the rear window.

Lily suppressed a laugh, and pulled the car into a lookout area. They all got out, and Jack quickly walked to the rock-walled rim to view the unobstructed panorama of green rolling mountains in the golden light of late afternoon.

"Go straight up the road," she messaged in her mind to the Fairies. "It's a big log house, facing west, with a yellow seven-pointed star on a flag in the front yard. At least, there used to be."

"We'll find it," the Fairies said and flew off into the tree line.

"After the flat terrain in Florida, this is a feast for the eyes," Jack said.

Lily inhaled the clean, pine-scented mountain air. "Now I'm home again."

Chapter 5

THE TOP OF THE WORLD

As they entered the deep forest, Runawind and Melarose came upon three Does, sipping creek water.

"Hello," Melarose softly said next to one of their ears. The Doe turned her head to the right and Melarose flew in front of her big, luminous brown eye. The Doe made a soft sound of welcome.

"We are new here," Melarose said as Runawind joined her. "We're headed way up the mountain to a house owned by a man named Will. Do you think we could get a ride?"

The Doe looked over at her companions and had a short, silent discussion. Deer are extremely telepathic—a talent that helps them travel together, undetected, through the woods.

"We know the place," the first Doe said. "The man is respectful, and doesn't hunt without need. We'll be happy to take you there. But we must go quickly, so we can be back down here before the sun sets. Hold on tight and stay right behind my head."

And with Runawind and Melarose clinging to the hairs on her neck, the Doe took off at a sprint. It was exhilarating for the Fairies to feel the rush of air and see the green trees, streaking by. They giggled so much that Runawind almost lost his grip. In a short while, they felt the Doe slowing down. All three Does stopped when they came to the edge of a tree line that bordered the large grassy area around a log house.

"We'll tell our friend you helped us," Melarose said, flying off the Doe's back to thank her. "I'm sure there will be a nice treat for you all if you wander up here in a day or so."

The Doe replied with a short satisfied snort. Then she and her companions turned, and quickly disappeared back into the woods.

"This is it," Runawind said, fluttering near the flag. A breeze held the flag open to reveal a seven-pointed yellow star above two curved laurel branches on a white background. It was an emblem of the Cherokee Nation.

"Runawind...listen," Melarose whispered.

"Hey hi hi ya, hey hi yo. The top of the world is the place to go. Hey hi hi ya, hey hi yay. I am the Keeper of the Way." The voice singing out of sight on the far side of the house was deep and gruff.

"I think...," Runawind began.

"It's an Elf," Melarose finished his thought for him.

Whether this was a good or a bad thing depended on the Elf's mood and nature. The song, which he continued to repeat, didn't sound threatening, so they flew to the corner of the house and peeked around the side.

"Ho there. Come around where I can see you well." The Elf's statement startled them. "Fairies," he groaned in a mock serious way. "Always seem to think they have it over on the rest of us." This was followed by a big belly laugh.

They flew to the back of the house and saw a stocky man, about two feet high, with twinkling green eyes and a long, grizzled black beard. He wore a suit in a hodgepodge of fabrics, likely made from garments 'borrowed' from a clothesline. His shoes were certainly fine, made of deerskin and decorated with bits of shell and bone. On his head was a small red and white Santa cap, probably taken from a child's discarded toy. But this was pierced around the back rim, with small bird feathers of many colors.

Melarose thought it would take quite a while to properly take in all the aspects of this Elf's costume. Not wanting to appear rude, Melarose cut her observations short and introduced them both. "And who are you?" she ventured to ask.

The Greatest Enchantment

"Who am I? Did you not hear? The Keeper of the Way," he intoned, then laughed again. "But my friends call me Plenty Birchbark, and I guess you can call me that, too—though no one knows my secret name."

"Of course not," Runawind said, to convey his respect for the Elf way. "But can you tell us the reason for your friendly name?"

"Oh, I do a fair amount of shaping with the pieces of birch bark that peel off the trees near the creek. Sometimes a hiker, or the man who lives here, finds a piece with a recognizable shape and thinks it's an amazing thing. And all the time, it's been done by me, and for my own amusement." Plenty jiggled and roared with laughter.

"Are you always at this house?" Melarose asked him. She knew that Elves often had one home they protected or plagued, depending on how well they liked the owner.

"Yes—if I'm not on an adventure in the woods. I keep watch over things. Will here's a good man and keeps some of the old ways, too," Plenty said. "He remembers to leave the Spirit Plate out at almost every meal, and he's not a bad cook, either." At this thought he did a little dance to display his pleasure. Faeries liked a Spirit Plate, too. It held small, best bits of a person's meal. Those who knew the value of this practice left it outside their home to honor the Nature Spirits and court their good will.

"Do you know Lily, Will's niece?" Runawind asked.

"Ah, the lovely child—the one who left us." Plenty sighed.

"Well, she's back," Runawind said. "You'll be seeing her up here in a day or two."

"That will do me and the old man a world of good," Plenty said with a big grin. "A world of good. It's lonely for him now that he's retired, and with his children and wife all gone." The tear that fell from Plenty's eyes told the Fairies how much he had loved and missed these people, too. "Is she back to stay?"

"We aren't sure," Melarose said, and proceeded to tell the Elf why they were here, and at his insistence, a particularly long version of their own adventure in the Land that Has No Fall. Elves love a good tale as much as any Fairy. Before she had begun, Plenty had insisted on sitting down on a tree stump and lighting the little corn husk pipe he had packed with leaves, so he could listen at leisure.

By the time Melarose finished and Runawind had added a few of his own opinions, the sun had set. When the Elf began to comment on the tale, he was interrupted by the sound of wheels crunching on the gravel drive, and the flash of headlights.

"He'll be home," Plenty said and danced a little jig.

The man parked his truck at the back door. When he got out, the Fairies were impressed by the height and apparent strength of a human some years past his prime. The arms, visible below the short sleeves of his black T-shirt, were muscular, and his jeans were belted with a shining silver buckle in the shape of an eagle's head. A thumb-sized brown suede pouch hung from his neck. He wore his gray-streaked, straight black hair pulled back in a long braid, and topped with a broad-brimmed hat of finely worked brown deerskin. The hat band, a weave of brown, yellow and green, created a place to tuck a randomly found feather. Today, there were wing feathers of blue jay and turtle dove. His clean-shaven face carried a hint of beard-shadow, and his dark brown eyes carried shades of sorrow.

The Fairies took turns flying in front of him and were disappointed when he didn't notice them. The man clearly had his mind on getting the two big bundles, propped up in the flat bed, into the house. Maybe that was why.

"No," Plenty said. "He doesn't see us. He did when he was a boy, though, before the church folk told him he was a fool. His mother sees us, still. So does that lovely young girl, Lily. But he puts the Spirit Plate out anyway, just in case." Plenty was all smiles.

"That's sad," Melarose said. "And he seems sad, too."

"He'd know he isn't alone if he could see us," Runawind added.

"Well, it hasn't been for lack of me trying," Plenty roared with laughter, remembering some of his antics to call attention to himself. "And I've left him a fair amount of birch bark shapes, too…even one that was a pretty good image of me, in all my glory. But he seems lost in his thoughts most of the time, and I know they have much to do with his younger days."

The Greatest Enchantment

The telephone began to ring and the man rushed inside, carrying the two brown paper bags, leaving the door open. The curious Fairies and Elf rushed in behind.

Quickly dropping the bags on the kitchen table, he lifted the old fashioned trim line receiver. "Hello?" he asked. He wasn't used to getting phone calls. The Fairies hovered next to his ear, hoping to hear who was on the line.

"Uncle Will? It's Lily. I'm here. I'm home." Lily said in a breathless rush.

"Lily?" Will's question sounded as if he thought he was dreaming.

"Yes, it's me. I'm staying in Cherokee tonight. I would love to see you tomorrow. Is that okay?"

"Of course," Will said. "Come for lunch. Do you remember how…"

"I do. I can see your house as clear as day," Lily cut him off, so grateful to hear his invitation. "Can I bring a friend with me? We drove back up here together."

"I'll be happy to meet anyone who brought you home to us," Will said.

"Thank you! We'll be there by noon. Right now, we're grabbing some dinner and I need to get to bed…it was a long drive up."

"Yes. You rest now, Lily. Should I call your Granny?"

"No. Thank you. I'd better do that myself in the morning." Will heard the hesitation in her voice.

"She loves you child. We all do. You just get a good rest tonight. All will be well," he promised.

"Thank you Uncle Will. I love you, too. Bye now," Lily said. The Fairies knew she was probably crying.

Will placed the receiver back in its cradle. He sat down, propped his elbows on the table, put his hands over his face and cried, too.

"He's happy, he's happy," Plenty shouted incongruously, dancing his sprightly jig. The Fairies looked at him, confused. "Really, he is. Can't you see those sparks of joy playing around his heart? I haven't seen them in a very long time."

And when the Fairies flew in front of Will, they saw that there were, indeed, ribbons of golden light dancing in front of his chest. They decided to leave him to his private emotions and flew back out into the yard.

There, they found the darkness was intermittently lit by fireflies, and the steady glow of lamplight coming from the kitchen. Melarose yawned.

"We can ask those ferns if they'll give up a leaf or two. That, and a bit of moss from the side of those rocks over there, will make you a snug spot in the small hole up in that oak tree." Plenty pointed to a large old tree across from the back door. "It used to have a family of wrens living in it, but they moved further downhill to another yard. The woman there has many full bird feeders and lots of hollow gourds for nesting, hung high up with barbed wire so the snakes can't reach," he said. The sleepy Fairies eagerly agreed both to his plan, and the wisdom of the wrens.

"Thank you, Plenty," Melarose called down from inside the snug hole when their Fairy Beds were made. "We're so glad we met you." With that, she was fast asleep.

"We are," Runawind said. "I wish you a good night."

Plenty doffed his cap at him, revealing a shining bald pate as he bowed. "At your service," he said, and then danced off to the side of the house where he began to sing.

"Hey hey yo, hey yo hey hey. Night has overcome the day. Hey hi yo, hi hey hey yo. So it's off to sleep I go."

With a satisfied smile, Runawind joined Melarose in the world of dreams.

"You see? You see?" Plenty's booming voice and hearty laugh shook both Fairies from their slumber. They fluttered to the edge of their snug hole, looked down to see Plenty, pointing at a paper plate on the ground. On it was pieces of pancake, some scrambled eggs, and a piece of bacon. "Better get down here quick if you want to sample Will's fine cooking," Plenty said. "By the sound of it, the Crow family has gotten wind of this— and we'll need to leave them some." And sure enough, they could hear loud crow calls going back and forth as the big black birds decided who would lead their family down to the yard.

Melarose and Runawind hastened to enjoy a Fairy-sized feast. Plenty took a few good gobbles of pancake, let out a big, satisfied belch and said, "Here they come." The three quickly left the plate to the four crows that landed with a chorus of squawking. The birds fought heartily over the last of the breakfast, especially the long piece of bacon. As crows do, they enjoyed this haggling. They knew all along their father would break this bacon slice up and take the biggest piece for himself. He sat with his prize in a low branch now, tasting and biting off small pieces, at his leisure. The haggling was meant to make his victory all the sweeter, and he knew his family all had something to satisfy them, too.

Melarose would have gone to introduce herself to him, but she was aware that while a crow eats, it has no time for pleasantries.

"Come on. I'll show you some of the forest. We'll be back in time to see the reunion when Lily arrives," Plenty offered.

And so the rest of the morning was spent meeting the plants and creatures of the land surrounding Will's house. This restored the Fairies even more than their long night's sleep. Along with Plenty, they were engaged in spirited conversation with two dragonflies and a bumblebee about how dangerous it was in The Land That Has No Fall, when they suddenly heard Lily's mind. She was worrying about how Uncle Will would feel about Jack.

"Our friends are here," Runawind said in mid-sentence. "I hope we'll see you again." Proper apologies were made all around, and they eagerly flew off to greet Lily.

By the time the blue SUV was in front of the house, Will was walking down the wide porch steps, waving them in. He had chosen to wear a bright turquoise T-shirt today. Along with his pouch, a string of jet and turquoise beads hung around his neck. In the daylight, the Fairies got a good look at the tanned, handsome, though somewhat lined face, that was now smiling.

Lily jumped out of the car and ran into Will's arms. He lifted her off her feet in a great hug that seemed it would go on for a while, till Jack coughed, indicating his presence.

"Oh, I'm sorry Jack," Lily said, on the ground now and out of the hug, but with an arm still around her uncle's waist. "This is my Uncle Will. Uncle, this is my friend, Jack Lerner."

"Pleased to meet you, young man," her uncle said, extending his hand. Despite his pleasant greeting, the Fairies could see him sizing Jack up and making some quick decisions. It appeared that Uncle Will was one of the members of her family Lily could count on for wise counsel.

Jack saw this, too, and was well aware that 'young man' was meant to put him in his place, right away. He smiled broadly and shook Will's hand with a strong grip. "My honor, sir," he said.

"Take a look around the yard if you like," Will offered, knowing the view was spectacular, even if he had let the garden go a bit. "Then come on inside. I've got something cooking." He hugged Lily again, and went into the house, leaving the two young folks to do as they wished.

"Isn't it beautiful?" Lily asked, extending her arm out at the view of the mountains to the west.

"Incredible," Jack replied. His mind could not help calculating the price of homes he could build, up on this site. He winced as felt another patch take hold on his other ankle. He'd kept his socks on for the massage last night, so he wouldn't scare the therapist. If he got many more patches, he'd have to leave his pants on next time. He sighed. Lily mistook this for the positive effect the view had on his spirit.

"I know. I used to sigh looking at this view, too. Wait till you see the sunset here," she said, and began walking around the property. She was thinking she might be able to help Uncle Will get his vegetable garden going again—do some pruning, fertilizing, and weeding. She wondered if Jack would help.

Runawind and Melarose decided it was time for them to make an appearance. They asked Plenty to stay hidden till Lily was alone, explaining that Jack didn't see Nature Spirits and Lily would want to greet him properly. That's when they remembered Lily's telepathy was working, too, and they looked over to see her quizzical expression. Runawind fluttered over and sat on her shoulder.

"We met an Elf," Runawind said. "He lives here. And he's really nice, too."

"Plenty?" Lily thought.

The Greatest Enchantment

"That's right," Melarose said, joining Runawind on Lily's shoulder.

"And if you have any apples, there are a few Does that we promised a treat," Runawind said.

"They gave us a ride up here," Melarose explained.

"Okay—will do. I've enjoyed my first massage and had a good night's sleep," Lily thought, filling them in. "And I called Grandma Rainmaker this morning."

"How did that go?" Melarose asked.

"She wants me there this afternoon." Lily answered, all the while looking as if she were inspecting the overgrown vegetable patch. "She sounded serious, but it didn't feel like she was angry with me."

"Do you want us to come with you?" Runawind asked.

"She said to come alone. But she just meant Jack, I'm sure." Lily thought. "Yes, it could be helpful to have you along," she decided. "Thank you."

Turning to Jack, she asked. "What do you think?"

Jack was trying hard not to think. He was afraid his real-estate-developer mind would take over. "It's beautiful. The yard needs some work of course. The porch could use some sanding, new paint and shellac. I wonder what the inside looks like," he said, gazing at the two story log home that he thought might have four or more bedrooms.

"Well, let's go and see," Lily said. They walked up the front steps that creaked a bit under their weight, opened the screen door, and entered Will's home. The curious Fairies still rode Lily's shoulder.

"Hello! Uncle Will?" Lily called from the front of the house.

"Back here," he called to them.

"Oh, it smells so good," she exclaimed, entering the kitchen. Uncle Will had prepared a big, welcome home, southern mountain lunch for them. A sugared ham roast rested on the countertop, pots of collards and butter beans simmered on the stove, and she detected the unmistakable scent of cornbread baking.

Will saw Jack closely inspecting the kitchen and rocking a little on his heels; a sign of impatience. "It'll be a little while before we're ready. Lily, you can help, while Jack here takes a look at the rest of the house."

"Sure," Lily said. "Jack you go on, but please don't take too long. I can't wait to dig into this meal." She turned to smile at Uncle Will. "Thank you for this," she said.

"Wish I'd picked up dessert when I was in town yesterday... these will have to do," Will said, producing a bowl of shiny red apples.

"Perfect," said Lily, for more than one reason.

Runawind followed Jack into the hallway. He wanted to observe and report back to Melarose and Lily if anything odd happened while Jack was, seemingly, alone.

Jack was pleased by what he found in the dining room, just across the hall from the kitchen. A large oval oak table, set for three, had a matching sideboard with shelves holding stacks of blue and white patterned dishes, while unknown items were stored in closed cupboards below. A pewter vase full of fresh wildflowers was on the serving area. Near the kitchen door, three instruments hung on the wall: a guitar, fiddle and banjo. Below them, a low coffee table held a dulcimer whose black lacquered base shone with a border pattern of gold leaf. Shellacked log walls held no paintings or other decoration. The double windows on the east wall looked out on the forest area that bordered the property. They were framed by pulled-back curtains in an unusual pattern of blue feathers on a white background.

A dark maroon carpet continued on into the next room which was reached through an open archway. It was a large living room, containing stuffed fabric couches and chairs, all in cornflower blue. There was pine furniture in this room, including a coffee table, strewn with magazines, some end tables with low white-shaded, round-based brass lamps and a small stack of gray stone coasters. The double-wide, floor to ceiling bookcase held objects as well as books. A grey fieldstone fireplace was on the southern wall. Its mantel was loaded with framed photos and more freshly picked local wildflowers. A wide picture window on the west wall overlooked the porch and the fantastic view.

The curtains were of the same fabric as the ones in the dining room. Jack imagined they were rarely closed. There was one notable piece of furniture missing; an entertainment center. Jack wondered why there was no TV and no sound system. These rooms were all clean, neat and decorated in good country style, but—except for the flowers clearly picked for this visit—the rooms looked and felt as if Will wasn't in them often, if at all.

Across the hallway, on the north side of the house was the master bedroom and bath. Jack smiled at the feminine bedspread on a queen-sized brass bed—pink and cream-colored roses on a pine-green background, echoed in the drapes framing large double windows that looked out at the mountains. To Jack, this meant that Will could not bear to change the way his wife had left this room. He caught this thought in time, and no new patch of scales formed from ideas of how to manipulate Will through knowing this weak spot. He glanced around at the dark cherry-wood furniture, walked over to the dresser, and looked at the lovely young woman in the gold oval frame. He hadn't stopped to inspect the other photos he'd passed, so he was surprised to see a light-skinned face with blue eyes, surrounded by long, wavy blonde hair.

On the way back toward the kitchen, was a guest bathroom with ice-blue walls, slate-gray tiles, blue and white-flowered shower curtain, and all-white and chrome furnishings. And last, there was a locked door next to the kitchen, that might have led into an office or a storage space. His curiosity was piqued by this. He thought maybe he'd find out what was in there at lunch. Or he'd ask Lily, later.

He was thinking this as he and his unknown Fairy escort re-entered the kitchen where Lily and her uncle were laughing at stories from old times.

"You have a lovely home, Will," he said.

"Four more bedrooms and two baths upstairs," Will said proudly. "You and Lily are welcome to stay here if you like."

"Are you sure?" Lily asked.

"It would make me very happy if you did," Will replied. "There's a lot of space going to waste with just me here now."

Lily turned to Jack. Her big smile was her answer.

"Sure," Jack responded to her unspoken question. "That's a very nice offer, Will. Thank you."

"Great—that's settled then. Stay as long as you like. Now, I believe we're ready to eat," Will said, handing the platter of sliced ham to Jack.

"I'm so happy," Lily thought to Melarose and Runawind. "Even though I'm sure it's partly because he can keep an eye on me this way, and get a good look at Jack, too."

"It's good to be loved and cared for by such a wise man, Lily," Melarose said, looking meaningfully at Runawind, whose cheeks turned bright pink. They laughed a soft, tinkling Fairy Laugh. The sound made Lily's smile even brighter, as she set the plate of warm, fragrant cornbread on the dining table.

The food was delicious and Jack thought the conversation went really well. That is, until he asked about the locked room. Will became serious and silent. Lily seemed to lose her peaceful composure, too.

"I'm sorry," he said quickly. "Wrong question."

"It's all right Jack," Will said amiably. "Not your fault. I told you to look around. I should be willing to answer your question."

"Uncle Will...," Lily began.

Will continued. "There are things in that room that my father gave me; things I remember having as a boy; things my wife didn't approve of much, being a Christian, and all."

"Will's father kept the old ways, Jack," Lily said.

"I'd like to hear about them," Jack ventured.

"Maybe sometime," Will replied, and returned to his quiet contemplation.

"People are interested in these things now," Lily told Jack. "They weren't, back then." Her tone implied that this was an understatement. "I'm going to clear the table—will you help me?"

Jack got up, grabbed the platter and a serving bowl, while Lily carried the collected dishes. He followed her into the kitchen and when she'd filled the sink with soapy water she said, "Grandfather Rainmaker was a powerful man. He carried big medicine, as they say here. It was hard for him when Will turned away from his teachings and let his wife stop him from coming to circles. I guess you saw her picture?"

"Yes," Jack admitted.

"There were a lot of feelings about these things, on both sides."

"He loved her very much," Jack said.

"How can you tell?" she asked.

"The bedroom looks like she's still sleeping there," Jack replied. "By now, most men I know would have ditched the bedspread and had something a bit more…"

"Masculine?" Lily laughed.

"Right," Jack laughed, too.

It was a nice moment between them. It reminded Lily of conversations between Melarose and Runawind.

"Don't jump to conclusions, but don't lose hope," Runawind's voice said in her mind. If cautious Runawind felt he could soften toward Jack a little now, that made her feel even better.

"Would you take the apples in, Jack? Ask Uncle Will if he wants me to make coffee."

Jack took the big blue bowl, and went back into the dining room.

Lily sighed, and started scraping the dishes and loading them into the soapy water in the sink.

"It is going well," she thought. "Almost too well. You're right Runawind. I won't rush into believing this is the way it will always be, but I hope that we are having a good effect on him."

"It does seem that way now," Runawind said. "But I think I'll stay behind while you and Melarose go to your Grandma's. I'll see more when he's alone with Uncle Will."

"Thank you," she smiled at the restless Fairy, who couldn't help blowing some soap bubbles into the air so he could fly around them and poke them with his fingers. "Careful now," she teased, pulling the stopper out, laughing when Runawind jumped at the loud sound of soapy water getting sucked down the drain.

Back in the dining room, everyone was happy to return to a light conversation mode. Will had just asked Jack about his properties in Florida when Lily finished her coffee and said, "Excuse me, but I better go now if I want to be back in time for dinner. May I take a few apples with me?" she asked. Will nodded and she turned to Jack. "Is it all right if I leave you here with Uncle Will?"

"Sure. You go on—don't worry about us," he smiled.

She smiled back.

"Don't forget to say 'hello' to Plenty before you go," Runawind whispered. He heard Lily agree, but all his attention was now on watching Melarose follow her out of the house. He realized this would be the first time they would be apart, for more than a short while, since their trip to The Land That Has No Fall. Melarose felt his spirits drooping, so she turned, waved, and sent him a big Fairy Beam Smile. Restored to good humor, Runawind imagined the cozy burrow he would find for them when they got back to Grandfather Mountain.

Melarose brought Lily to the exact spot the Deer had left them off. Lifting an apple to her lips, Lily whispered 'thank you,' before placing it on the ground, just inside the tree line. When she'd done this two more times, she heard a rustle in the brush and spied the three Does a short way off. One snorted, and all three twitched to signal their recognition and acceptance of her gifts.

"Hey di de, hey di do. It's off to Grandma's house you go. Hey di do, hey do de. Please stop first and talk with me." Lily went around the corner to the south side of the house and saw the Elf doing a sprightly jig, which he kept up till he heard the welcome sound of his young friend's laughter.

"It's so good to see you again, Plenty," Lily said.

"An even greater good, it is, for us to see you here again," Plenty replied. "The rain will fall now that you're here."

Lily was touched by this. She knew his words meant that everything was in order, and they could all be happy now. "Thank you for watching over Uncle Will all these years," she said. She took the last shiny red apple out of her pocket and handed it to him. This started Plenty jigging again, and she laughed and said, "I'm due at Grandma's, but I will be seeing a lot of you, now that I am going to be staying here."

"It's a blessing and the answer to all my wishes. Will has been in need of late. And I see there are many changes on the way for you all." That said, he pointed toward the SUV and sang, Hey yo hi, hey hi yo. Off to Grandma's house you go. Hey yo hi, hey hi yay. Now you must be on your way." He kept this song going till she was in the car and started the ignition.

Driving off, Lily looked in the rear view mirror and saw Plenty, pushing his apple prize behind the lilies. Then, she caught a glimpse of her own happy eyes. She felt so much love here on the mountain. How could she have missed feeling that before? She thought of Grandma Rainmaker, wondering what kind of reception she would have when she arrived at the small house in the woods.

"Lily, slow down or you'll miss your turn," Melarose warned.

"Sorry, I was remembering how I left here years ago, and wondering...," Lily began.

"Wondering is not worthwhile. Creating is." Melarose cut in.

"Creating?"

"What do you want to see?"

"I want Grandma to take me in her arms and welcome me home. I want her to understand, and forgive me."

"Then see that ahead of you. And be grateful for it. You know how that works," Melarose giggled.

"I do—you're right. How did you know this was the turn I had to take?" Lily asked.

"I see the golden rays of power coming down the road. They form a strong protection for her, alone here in the woods." Melarose said. "I'm looking forward to meeting this powerful Medicine Woman."

As Lily steered the car down the sloping driveway, she saw Grandma come around from the creek-side area behind the simple, one-story wooden house. She noticed Grandma's hands brushing over her skirts, and knew that meant she had gone to the creek to say her prayers.

Melarose giggled and said, "She has been creating, too."

Grandma walked toward the car. The minute Lily's door closed behind her, she felt herself in the warm embrace she'd hoped for.

"Child, it is so good to see you home again," Grandma said, wiping a tear from her eye. "Come inside. I have some cool herb tea for you, and a special treat."

Walking arm-in-arm, they entered the house, with Melarose following close behind. It was almost the way Lily remembered it, with just a few changes to reflect the years.

This one big room held the kitchen, dining area, and living room space, with a large stone fireplace whose hearth opened both into the living room and the small bedroom beyond. Grandma had changed the cushions on the chairs at the table, and on her most prized possession—an oak rocking chair, handed down from her own grandmother. Their deep-green fabric echoed the pine trees and the shiny leaves of blooming rhododendron bushes, visible through the windows on the far side of the room. The big, cozy couch and arm chair still had their fabric of autumn leaves on a brown background. A hooked rug in beige, rust and brown, that she'd helped Grandma make many years ago, covered the wooden floor between the coffee table and the fireplace. She gratefully inhaled the lingering smell of sage, tobacco, and the herbs used to make the tea.

"It's so good to be here," Lily said.

"Who is your little friend there?" Grandma asked, setting a glass down and pointing to Melarose.

"Sorry ... I'm used to being the only one who can see her." Lily said. "This is my dear friend, Melarose. Melarose, this is my Grandmother, Sarah Rainmaker."

Melarose fluttered a moment before Grandmother's face, taking in the deep pools of wisdom from her dark brown eyes. Waves of bright green flowed around Grandma, showing her love of nature and all creatures in every dimension. She fluttered up to Grandma's soft round cheek and planted a special Fairy Kiss there. Grandma smiled.

"If this lovely Fairy travels with you, there must be a big story here," Grandma said. She sat down and lifted a cover off a dish to reveal Lily's favorite cinnamon apple cake. Satisfied with the big grin this got, she began cutting her a generous slice.

"There is definitely a story," Lily said. "But first, I want to..."

The Greatest Enchantment

"There's no need to explain, child. I was young once, too. I can remember how I felt living here back then," Grandma said. "But then I met your Grandfather, and all that changed for me. I discovered the beauty of a life lived in harmony with the natural world around me. I felt the power of the old ways. I was one of the few lucky ones."

"But the way I left...," Lily began.

"Yes. That was wrong. And you will need to apologize to your former boss about that," Grandma said. "But you wrote us, and called a few times. We missed you, of course, but at least we knew where you were, that you were safe, so we weren't afraid for your life. And I had faith in you." She reached across the table and covered Lily's hand with her own. "Those who know the child know the adult."

Lily couldn't help herself, and began to cry. Grandma held her hand till she stopped.

"There now," Grandma said. "Eat your cake, and tell me how you came home with a Fairy friend—and with a man you called Jack?"

The next hour was spent telling the story. Since Grandma could hear her, Melarose started with the decision made on Midsummer's Eve, and how she and Runawind met Lily. They were both surprised when Grandma started laughing. "Jack was turned into a lizard?" she said, and laughed again.

It was hard for Melarose and Lily to think of it with humor, but Grandma's laugh was infectious and not a bit cruel. Soon the small home was filled with the laughter of all three. Melarose saw the rainbows of light this created and guessed that was the real reason behind Grandma's response. Lily was now visibly more relaxed, and her natural pink energy was growing stronger.

"Well—and what happened on the way up here?" Grandma asked when they'd all settled down again.

Lily told the rest of the story with her pink light beaming brightly. When she was up-to-date, including Lily's recent meeting with Plenty Birchbark, Grandma got up and brought the pitcher of herb tea over to the table. She poured two glasses, putting a small amount in the bowl of her spoon for Melarose.

"I'll look forward to meeting Jack," Grandma said. She took a long sip of the fragrant herbal blend, leaned back, and said, "But now, there are some things I must tell you."

Back at Will's house, Runawind was paying close attention to the conversation going on at the dining table. He enjoyed watching the spiraling colors and occasional sparks the two men were sending out. There was a billowing cloud of deceptive yellow-green with several aggressive red streaks around Jack, as he downplayed the extent of his involvement in developing land. A rolling wave of wisdom blue, carrying smudges of depressing brown, surrounded Will as he explained how his wife had inherited this house and the property from her father, shortly after they married. The brown areas increased when Will told Jack about his sons, especially the eldest one, who became a career Army man after serving in Afghanistan.

"Do you have any kids, Jack?" Will asked.

"Not that I know of," Jack said, expecting a laugh, but getting none.

"Ever married?"

"I came close a couple of times, but no," Jack admitted. "Until very recently, I've been too involved in business, and the travel I do, to think about settling down."

"What's changed?"

Jack couldn't help laughing at that question. "I think I'd better let Lily tell you about that."

"I'm her uncle—I need to ask." Will paused. "What's the relationship between you two?"

It wasn't as though Jack hadn't expected this question—what he didn't expect was being at a loss to answer.

"She's my friend," he finally said. "A very good friend. We're not romantically involved, if that's what you want to know." He felt unusually unsettled under Will's quiet, steady gaze.

Runawind was surprised, but glad to see dark blue floating in the usual yellow-green around Jack as he said this. He wasn't lying.

"Why don't we take a drive around? I'm sure you'd like to see more of this area than the inside of my house." Will laughed. Jack sighed involuntarily as the pressure eased.

The Greatest Enchantment

"I certainly would," he answered. "Lily took me to the lookout on the road up to your place. We also stopped at a waterfall, on our way into town."

"There's lots of falls around here," Will said. "Lots of lookouts, too. We'll see where the wind takes us."

The two men rose from the table, and it was time for Runawind to make a quick decision. Should he go with them, or stay here in case Lily and Melarose returned? He thought Jack would remain on his best behavior and keep his land development instincts under control. He didn't expect Will to give up any secrets, or act as anything other than a genial tour guide. So, Runawind followed the men outside, watched them drive off, and fluttered off to find Plenty. He wanted to continue his own explorations of this area.

He found the Elf, not far off, in a small clearing in the woods, humming a sweet, melodious tune and working on a piece of birch bark, that was about a foot high. Plenty was using a sharp piece of shiny obsidian that had been set into a notch in a thick twig and bound with leather strips, to create a knife of sorts, to cut the outline of his design.

"This piece is not too dry, but you've got to be very careful," Plenty said, acknowledging his friend. "You can still cause the bark to crack, and that would ruin the idea."

As Runawind quietly watched, the birch bark began to form a very interesting image, indeed.

Chapter 6

MOUNTAIN SONG

Lily and Melarose returned to the house to find that Jack and Uncle Will were still out roaming. Runawind was nowhere to be seen.

"I guess this is a perfect time to call Momma," Lily said, picking up the receiver in the kitchen. Melarose hovered nearby for moral support.

The phone at the shop rang and rang. Just as she was about to hang up, she heard her mother's voice say, "Cherokee Traders. Can I help you?"

"Momma, it's Lily. I'm here at Uncle Will's," she said. Hearing no reply, she added, "Where do you want to have dinner tonight?"

"I can't really talk now—shop's busy. Let's meet up at Double B Barbecue. Know where it is?"

"I think so. How many are coming?"

"Just your brother and me."

"Uncle Will, too, I hope," Lily said. "We'll be staying here."

"Oh. I guess that's good." There was brief silence. "Did you see your Grandma?"

"Yes."

"Okay. We'll see you at 6:30."

"Okay, Momma. See you then."

Lily replaced the receiver, walked out the kitchen door, and sat on the top step of the small back porch. She thought about what her Grandmother had told her. And she realized that her mother wasn't just busy in the store. Momma must be worried about what Lily might know. She let out a big sigh.

"Don't worry, Lily," Melarose said, landing on her knee. "So far, everything has worked out well. Jack will be able to handle this, too."

"Will he?" Lily sighed again. "You're probably right. But can I?"

Lily pictured her Grandma's strong, gnarled hands, reaching out to hold hers over the kitchen table—the tears forming as she began to speak. It made her own heart ache to see Grandma cry, even before she heard what Grandma had to say. And it shouldn't have been a surprise to find out that another young man in her family had fallen into trouble with the wrong kind of friends. But this was different. This was Billy.

Lily remembered the day Momma brought Billy home from the hospital. She was seven years old and this tiny baby brother was like a new doll—but even better. She had fallen in love with his sweet, round face and the soft sounds he made. She didn't even mind when he cried and she could always soothe him. When he was a little older, she loved how his big brown eyes followed her as she moved around the room; how, when she looked at him, he'd break into a giggle. She never minded helping Momma take care of him. He was her special 'little man.'

But then, she became a teenager, eager to be off with her friends. And then, Father died. Again her heart ached, as she realized how selfish she had been—lost in her own emotions and her growing desire to leave home. Now she could clearly see the look on Billy's face back then and what it conveyed; how lost he was, and how much he needed her; how angry he was at being ignored. Then, she left—suddenly, with no goodbyes. She felt so ashamed at how selfish and self-focused she had been. Melarose placed soft fairy kisses on the few dry spots between the tears streaking down Lily's face.

Hearing the crunch of tires approaching, Lily quickly wiped her cheeks, and looked up, expecting to see Uncle Will's truck. Instead, it was an older model, black Ford pickup with a covered flatbed. It took her a minute to recognize the slim young man who got out on the driver's side. He was leaner and more muscular than she remembered, his face more chiseled. He wore his hair long now; in a ponytail wrapped in leather. His spotless white T-shirt topped tight blue jeans. He wore moccasins, and she saw a small leather bag, like Uncle Will's, hanging from his neck.

"Danny," she whispered. "Danny Two Hawks?"

"Lily—long time," he said, and walked slowly toward her. She rose and came down the wooden steps to meet him. "I heard you were back." He opened his arms, inviting her to hug him. She hesitated a moment, then stepped into his embrace.

Danny—comforting smells of leather, wood and sun-warmed skin; heart beating strong and fast. She remembered the crush she had on him, back in High School. He was two years older; not within her reach. They would talk when he came into the convenience store where she worked. One time, at a party, he'd asked her to dance. But they never had a date—never shared a kiss, or even a long hug, like this one. But he was here now, and she felt protected by his strong, quiet, inward presence. She wondered if he still made wood carvings of animals and bowls. He had given her a carved acorn one day, long ago.

"Let's walk," he said, breaking from the embrace. He took her hand and led her into the woods on a path that began behind the house. "Tell me how your life has been."

"There's a lot to tell, Danny," she said. "I'm not sure I can go into it all now. I hope you understand. But I'm back."

Hearing this, he stopped, and hugged her again. This time, she felt her own strong heartbeat meet his. The thought of Jack slipped into her mind. But there was no reason not to stand here, being held by Danny, soothed by his energy—as steady and strong as the tall trees they stood between.

"Lily!" a voice called, breaking her reverie.

"Lily?" It was Jack's voice this time.

She pulled herself out of Danny's arms. "They must be wondering where I disappeared to," she said. "Come meet my friend."

Danny held her hand as they walked the short distance back to the yard. Lily thought she should probably let go when they got within sight of the two men waiting there. But again, there really was no reason to do that.

"Jack, this is Danny Two Hawks—an old friend of mine," she said. As she spoke, Danny had reached out with his right hand to shake hands with her uncle. Now he did the same with Jack. Lily saw an odd look cross Jack's face. Was he jealous?

"Come on in," Uncle Will invited.

When they were all seated at the kitchen table with a cold sweet-tea before them, Lily asked Jack how he'd enjoyed the drive.

"This area is magnificent," Jack replied. He didn't mention that he'd felt a few patches of lizard skin form on his lower leg when they had visited several of the scenic views. How could he stop himself from seeing the beautiful mountains covered with upscale houses? He was definitely feeling torn by his natural instincts, and knowing how this was the opposite of what he needed to become if he wanted to stay in his human body. It frightened him that, if he even thought about this quandary for too long, he'd feel another patch claim its place on his leg. Now, here was Lily with this handsome young man. Why did he feel so awful about that—like something was being taken from him?

Lily sensed all of that—and more. But she saw Runawind, fluttering at the screen door. "I think I forgot something in the car," she said and got up to let Runawind come in as she went out.

"Melarose," Runawind cried, flying to her side. "You'll never guess what's happening."

"Neither will you." Melarose followed this with her sweet, twinkling laugh. They flew off to a corner of the room to catch up.

"So, how do you know Lily?" Danny asked. And that was the conversation Lily overheard as she came back into the kitchen. While she put the small bags of sage and loose tobacco Grandma had given her on the kitchen counter, she was listening to the story Jack was making up about how they were neighbors in Florida, and that he'd offered to drive her home, so he could see this area. Well, it wasn't totally untrue.

"And you, Danny," Jack asked. "What do you do around here?"

Lily heard more in this question than Jack was asking. Danny smiled and took a moment to answer.

"I'm a carpenter. I also carve. You'll find some of my pieces in the stores in town," Danny said.

"I have one here," Uncle Will said, getting up to fetch it.

"And you?" Danny asked Jack. He put his hand on Lily's back, who'd sat back down beside him.

Jack wanted to say something to show his greater wealth and establish his dominance over this situation, but opted to downplay instead. "I do some stuff with real estate."

"Hmmm," Danny replied.

"I spoke to Momma," Lily said, as Uncle Will returned and handed a beautifully detailed carving of a deer to Jack for his inspection. "She wants us to meet at Double B at 6:30. Danny? Would you like to have dinner with us?"

"Thanks, but I'd better be going," Danny said, downing his tea and rising. "Thanks, Will—nice to meet you, Jack."

"I'll walk you out," Lily said.

At the car he hugged her again. "I never forgot you."

"Danny..."Lily began.

"I'm glad you're home," he interrupted. Stepping back, he placed something in her palm, gently closing her fingers over it. He looked into her eyes, as though he was seeking something in their depths. "Your Grandma knows where to find me," he said. He got into the Ford and started the engine.

So Grandma told him I was here, Lily thought, watching him drive off. When she opened her fist, she found a carved acorn. Heat rushed into her face, as she suddenly realized the meaning of the gift, and the other acorn he'd casually given her one day long ago. If she had understood back then, would she have ever left Cherokee?

She jumped as the screen door banged shut behind her. Jack come down the steps and stood beside her now, looking down the road.

"It's really beautiful here, Lily," he said.

"I had forgotten just how beautiful," she sighed.

"I hope it never changes," he said.

She turned toward him in time to see the tear sliding down his cheek.

The Greatest Enchantment

Melarose and Runawind saw this tear, too. They looked at each other, told Lily they would be back, and left to find Plenty.

"What do you think?" Melarose asked as they fluttered along.

"Jack is finding it hard to stay in his usual personality," Runawind offered.

"Yes. He doesn't feel in control anymore," Melarose sighed.

"I like Danny," Runawind said.

"Of course," Melarose laughed. Just then, they heard the Elf singing nearby.

"Hey hi ya, hey hi hi. Birch bark message, time to fly. Hey hi hey, hey hi yo. Off to Lily's house you go." While Plenty repeated his song three times, Melarose gazed at the image he'd carved.

"How will Lily get to see it?" Melarose asked.

"Oh, don't you be worrying about that," Plenty said. "I have my ways." He began singing his song again. This time, it conjured a breeze that easily lifted the bark, and took it toward the back of the house. The Elf and Fairies followed close behind. After three more sets of his song and three more gusts of light wind, the Elf seemed pleased.

"Here?" Runawind pointed at the spot on the back porch where the bark had come to rest.

The Elf doubled over with laughter, and began to dance in a circle. Finally, he stopped.

"You'll see. The men have gone to the living room, hey?" Plenty asked. When the Fairies peeked into the kitchen and agreed that they had, he continued, "Lily has come to the kitchen alone now, for a glass of water." Yes, they saw Lily was there, getting a glass out of the cabinet. "Watch," he told them. "Hi yi fly!"

At this, the birch bark lifted, flew up to the door, and tapped on the screen. They saw Lily turn. The bark tapped again. Lily looked down to see something, fluttering against the screen door. She carefully opened the door, and stepped out onto the porch. Another light breeze brought the bark to her feet. Birch was a wisdom tree and a healer, Grandma Rainmaker had told her, and one should not take a piece of its bark without asking if it was for them. But she hadn't any need of it, so she just reached down, picked it up, gently tossed it into the grass in the yard, and returned to the kitchen.

Melarose and Runawind looked at the Elf, who was hugging himself to keep from laughing out loud. "Watch," he told them again. "Hi yi, fly!" he whispered.

And up the bark went and tapped on the door again. Lily came out quickly now, her brow furrowed with curiosity. She lifted the bark once more. This time she spoke to it. "You came back. Are you for me?" Apparently, the bark said 'yes,' because she took it into the house, with the Fairies riding her shoulder. Plenty danced off to wait behind a nearby bush.

"What is it?" Melarose asked.

"I don't know, but it came back after I set it free. It must have something to tell me," Lily said. She began to study the piece of bark, turning it this way and that—suddenly, she made a sound of surprise. She'd just realized she was looking at the outline of a woman with arms held out to either side. On one open palm sat a lizard; on the other, an acorn. "Do you see it?" she asked the Fairies. Indeed, they did.

Lily went to get a pinch of tobacco from the bag on the counter. She went back outside, and stood on the porch, holding the bark against her heart. With her right hand, she brought the tobacco to her lips and whispered a prayer of thanks before she sprinkled it on the porch, in front of the screen door. From his hiding place, Plenty softly chuckled. His message had been received.

Re-entering the house, Lily quickly took the bark image upstairs. She scanned her bedroom for a place where she could see it often; a place that Jack wouldn't notice if he happened to come in. Nothing here seemed right, so she checked the bathroom. A small screened window was on the wall between the sink and the door. It had a view of the trees. She put the bark on the window ledge and stood back. Yes—that was perfect. Taking the carved acorn out of her jeans pocket, she placed it on the window ledge in front of its bark reflection.

"I'm going to have to choose," she said to the Fairies.

The Greatest Enchantment

"But not now," Runawind said.

"Not yet," Melarose agreed. "The arms of the woman spread out in an even line give no judgment."

"That's true." Lily touched the acorn again, for luck. She left her room, and returned to Jack and Uncle Will, waiting below.

Runawind and Melarose had opted to stay home while Will, Lily and Jack went to meet Rose and Billy for ribs at the Double B. When the SUV drove off, they decided to look for Plenty, and found him nearby, leaning against a tree trunk and smoking his tiny corncob pipe. He was admiring a perfect smoke ring, as it floated upwards, and getting ready to form another, when he noted the arrival of his Fairy friends.

"It's been a satisfying day," he said.

"Plenty," Melarose got right to the point. "Runawind said he found you carving that birch bark image, long before Danny came to the house."

"So I was, so I was," Plenty replied, tamping out the fire in his pipe and letting out a sigh. "Nothing like a good chicory chip smoke on a warm summer's eve."

"But how did you know? Danny gave Lily the acorn only as he was leaving," Runawind pressed the point.

"Well, you should know I have my ways. But, my little friends, here's the tale you're yearning for. Now listen well," he said. "Hundreds of years ago, my grandfather came to this country from over the great sea, with the family he watched over. A century after that, my father came here, with an eldest son, who chose to settle in these beautiful mountains. But, despite the hospitality of the native people who lived here, that family didn't fare well. First, the father perished on a hunting expedition. Then the wee ones caught a sickness and passed on. That left the wife all alone in her cabin near the mountain top." Plenty stood up to better tell his story, with all the dramatic gestures that might be necessary.

"One day, some men came up the mountain. They were strangers, just riding through the area on their way west; but they'd heard talk of the pretty dark-haired woman, alone in her home near the mountain top. They decided to stop by, thinking she might have a few things they would like to take before they left on their way; it would be easy, too, what with no one there to stop them, and all." Plenty paused for effect, and to enjoy the sight of the Fairies, with their eyes wide and mouths agape.

"What happened?" Melarose cried out, unable to stand the suspense.

"My father had made himself known around these parts and he'd made some friends, too—native people, who could see and speak to him. And so, when he'd got wind of the approach of these riders, he hurried off to get help. The first person he came upon was a young Cherokee man, out hunting for small game. When the riders arrived, they were surprised to be met by this strong young man, with a knife in his belt, his bow drawn, and an arrow aimed at them."

"What happened?" Melarose cried again.

Plenty laughed. "Why, absolutely nothing. The two horseman galloped back the way they'd come. When she heard them ride away, the woman came out from the house and threw her arms around the young man—so happy was she, that he had saved her. This young man had never before known a woman to do such a thing, but he felt curiously glad, being held by her. And when they stood apart and looked into each other's eyes, well, let's say the feeling took hold.

"Now you both know, coming from not so far away, that when the white folks arrived in this area, the native people took them in like brothers. They taught them what this rich land offered for survival. And the white men taught them some new farming ways, and offered them their own take on the Great Spirit. In those early days, it wasn't so odd to have a marriage take place between these people. And so it happened that, not long after this rescue, the young Cherokee man and the widowed Irish woman took each other for man and wife."

"And were they happy?" Melarose asked.

"As happy as two can be. And they had seven children of their own; all strong and able, all dark-haired like their parents—a few with sky-blue eyes, like their mother."

"But what does this have to do with Danny and Lily?" Runawind demanded. As impatient as ever, he had heard enough about the old days.

"As is the Elf tradition, my grandfather, and then my father after him, took guardianship of the oldest son and his family," Plenty said.

"So…Will is the oldest son of that family now?" Melarose asked, finally getting the drift.

"Indeed he is, as his father was before him," Plenty replied. "And so now, who do you think told me about Danny, then?"

"Grandma Rainmaker?" Melarose offered.

"None other," Plenty said. "I know when she calls out to me, and I search her mind for what she needs. I sometimes visit her house, too. I have so many happy memories of days there, when her husband was alive."

"She wanted you to give that message to Lily?"

"Oh no. That was my idea." Plenty lost himself for a moment in his full belly laugh. When he recovered, he said, "I've never seen them fail. But come—before you start asking any more questions, there's someone I want you to meet. The sun will be setting before too long and then she might be hard to find, and none too happy to be disturbed." He danced a short jig before he set off, with the Fairies riding his sturdy shoulders.

Before long, they entered the cool, green canopy of the deep forest. Only the beautiful melodies of birdsong—calling out their roosting place to the returning flock—interrupted the peaceful serenity. A bit further in, the Fairies were surprised to hear an unusual, deep, gravelly voice singing. The song was very similar to the one Plenty had been singing, when they first came upon him at Will's house.

"Hey hi hi ya, hey hi yo. To the mountain you must go. Hey hi hi ya, hey hi yay. Only love will lead the way. Only love will lead the way. Hey hi hi ya, hey hi yay."

The voice went on and on, singing the same words, and the same tune, as though it did so, perpetually.

"Yes," Plenty said. "That's her. We'll find her, presently."

When the voice was very close, Plenty stopped before what seemed a mass of tangled roots beneath an ancient oak tree. He doffed his cap, bending over in a low bow.

"Hey yo hey, hey yo hey. Plenty the Elf has come your way. Hey yo hi, hey yo hi. With his friends he's passing by," Plenty sang.

As the Fairies looked on, the clump of roots slowly began to move. A figure finally emerged, presenting a form that appeared almost human. If not for the great number of gnarled appendages issuing from its sides and legs, one might think an old, round woman sat cross-legged on the ground, with a mass of wild knots for hair, and an ancient face, deeply creased by innumerable years. Iridescent green lights with black oval centers looked like cat's eyes, whose pupils narrowed and widened, as they peered at Plenty and his Fairy companions.

The gravel voice seemed to come from the depths of the earth as it issued a greeting: "Hey ho, Elf. What mischief requires my presence?"

"Only the same as always, my Lady," the Elf said, bowing low again. "May I introduce my friends, as they are part of the story?"

The gnarled-one rumbled and shook with what must have been laughter. "He calls me 'Lady,'" the gravel voice finally said. "There is no invention in creation, perceived by the men the Elves serve, which is not given the image of a beautiful woman with long silky hair. And the closest Nature truly gets to that, is found inside an ear of corn." The rumbling laughter began again.

"Forgive me," Plenty added. "Indeed, it is a habit, handed-down."

"I am Runawind, and this is Melarose," Runawind began. "But what should we call you?"

The rumbling laughter stopped, the black ovals narrowed, appraising Runawind before giving an answer. "If you must call me something—and it appears you must—call me Singer of the Wood, for I give voice to the trees. They do not often need me, but for my song. When they do, and one appears who can hear me, I arise from my comfortable place at the foot of this great tree and engage my speaking facility, as I am doing now. Surely, you have such a Singer on your own mountain home?"

Runawind looked to Melarose. "We must," Melarose replied. "Maybe there has been no need for us to witness this before now."

The appearance of a head nodded, satisfied with this. Then the great green eyes looked back at Plenty, waiting for the full answer to the question.

"My friends have a story to tell you. But first, I hoped for you to hear me tell our own—so you might correct me, if there are any errors," he said, and bowed in deference once again. This seemed to meet with approval, and Plenty began speaking to the Fairies. "There came the dark time when the desires of the newcomers got the better of them, and they sought to take all the lands from the native people—the pastures for grazing, the waterfalls to power their mills, and their greatest desire of all, that which lay within the mountains—gold. Many friends turned their back on their native brothers, and allowed this to happen. Finally, the saddest day came when the native people were rounded up and held in the Fort. They would be forced to walk on a long journey, to a place far away in the west; but some refused to leave their beautiful mountain home, and thought to hide."

"I think I've heard of this from our History Tellers at the Festivals," Runawind put in.

"I was here at that time, protecting my family, and they were among the ones who wouldn't go," Plenty said. "Not that I blamed them, but I had a hard task ahead to hide them till the danger passed—if it would. Native scouts from other parts, and those who turned on their own tribe in order to keep their own selves safe, were wise trackers. They also knew most of the caves where people might choose to hide. And so, I came to the Singer of the Wood to ask for advice." Plenty paused, waiting for any correction to be made. Hearing none, he went on.

"I was fortunate to be given several Song Charms: one to make vines grow thick, and quick as a blink; and one to make water spring up from the ground. These, I shared with other families, who had made their way high into the mountains.

Another charm was given to me for my family—it opened a portal in this very tree, and would lead them to a sheltered valley, where they could not be found. And there they stayed—safe and undetected—until the sacrifice of one family was made, and a Commanding Officer kept his promise to leave all other runaways alone; a promise that was kept. But this is a story for another time."

"You mean to say, Will's great-grandfather and his kin went to the Otherworld, out of time?" Runawind asked.

"No. But it was a place very much like that. After this, Will's family knew how important it was to carry and keep the medicine line—and that's why Will's father married Sarah; a woman he cared for deeply, and who he knew would come to love the sacred ways," Plenty said. "So, you see, this family has long been bound, by promise and gratitude, to the Singer of the Woods."

"And this is why it was so painful for the Rainmakers when their son put the old ways aside for his bride," Melarose realized.

"It has been more painful for Will than anyone else," Plenty said. "No one can avoid suffering when they keep silent and shun a truth they know. Nor should a person have to be anything but who they truly are with one they love. But," the Elf brightened. "I think the time has come where all this can be brought around to a place where it can be made whole again. I seek the Singer's advice on how I should proceed." He bowed again at the gnarled figure. "But first, the Singer must hear your own story."

And so, to their delight, the Fairies were called upon to tell of their journey and why they were here now with Lily White Dove. It was very close to nightfall when they were done.

At first, the silence was penetrated only by the sound of crickets and frogs, competing with sporadic bird calls. Then, the tangled appendages seemed to straighten outward and the figure rose higher.

"Yes, this is the day the trees have whispered about for ages," the Singer bellowed. "Through all the wailing and the suffering of creatures and men all around us, through all the threats to our own lives, here in this wood, the trees have told that a great time would come. In that time, the long suffering would be healed, and all would hear the Song of the Mountain again. Hey hi hi ya, hey hi yo. To the Mountain you must go. Hey hi hi ya, hay hi yay. Only love will lead the way. Only love will lead the way. Hey hi hi ya, hey hi yay," the gravelly voice sang loud and strong. The Fairies saw the tree-tops bend toward them; the crickets, birds and frogs ceased their sounds. When the Singer was silent again, the Fairies felt a new vigor, infusing everything around them.

"Come closer, Elf," the Singer said. "We must decide how to begin."

Melarose and Runawind left the Elf and the Singer to their deliberations and made their own way back to Will's house. They were surprised to see two cars there—the SUV, and a white compact car with a few dents on the passenger side. But what caused them to stop and hide behind the head of a drooping sunflower was seeing the Shadow that lurked near the house. There was no other possibility but one—someone from this white car was an object of interest for the Shadow and it had not been able to attach to this desired host—yet.

Fluttering slowly backwards, the Fairies managed to make it up their tree and into their snug space without attracting the Shadow's notice. They peered over the edge toward the house. They could hear Lily's mother come out onto the porch, thanking Jack for dinner. As Lily, Jack and Will were saying their goodbyes, the screened door to the kitchen opened again.

A young man came out and started down the steps. The Fairies hadn't heard him say anything to anyone. His face was cast down, his shoulders hunched over a body that was lean, but appeared weak; his movements, slow and slightly unsteady. He was dressed in baggy jeans with holes at the knees, a wrinkled brown T-shirt, and sneakers whose laces had come untied. A beige cap with its brim pointing backwards, covered a mass of uncombed, shoulder length black hair, and there was a few day's growth of stubble on his sullen face. He quickly got into the passenger seat of the small white car and closed the door. Before it was completely shut, the Shadow slid into the car behind him.

"Call me soon," Rose said to Lily.

"I will Mamma," Lily replied. Her face showed no emotion, but the Fairies knew she was hiding fear and concern.

"We'll do it again," Jack said, shaking Rose's hand. "Have a good night."

"Goodnight Rose—safe home," Will said, and turned to go back into the house. Jack followed.

Rose appeared to want to linger, but as the men passed through the open screened door, she went to the car, got in and drove off. Lily remained on the porch to watch her go. The Fairies quickly fluttered down to her side.

"Was that your brother?" Runawind asked.

Lily's response was an outpouring of silent tears. She walked down the steps and around to the side of the house where she could talk to them out loud. A waxing crescent moon cast a soft illumination through the trees.

"Tell us," Melarose said, landing lightly on her shoulder.

"It's pretty bad," Lily said. "My brother dropped out of school, has no job, and I am guessing at the rest."

Runawind felt he had to tell her. "We saw a Shadow here, waiting for him to come out."

"Oh, no," Lily moaned. "What can I do? We have to stop it before it attaches to him."

"I see why your Grandma was so upset now, Lily," Melarose said. "But nothing can be done tonight—except to ask for the right help to come."

"Yes, that's it," Lily brightened. She went into the kitchen to retrieve the tobacco and sage for her prayers. Both Will and Jack sat quietly at the kitchen table, with concerned looks on their faces.

"What do you think?" Will asked her. "Jack here was talking about sending him off to one of those schools that can keep him in line, and prepare him for the military."

Lily looked at Jack. "You're very kind. I do appreciate the thought and your generosity—but right now we have to smudge this room to clear the bad energy. Then we must pray—Uncle Will?"

Will took a deep breath and exhaled slowly. "Okay," he said. "Wait here."

When he had gone, Jack took Lily's hand. "You've been so kind to me, Lily. I could never repay you for what you've done, no matter how I tried."

Lily's smile at these words became a look of astonishment when Uncle Will re-entered the kitchen. He was carrying two drums, a large shell and part of a vulture wing. Held in high regard by the Native people, who also called it 'thunderbird,' the vulture was said to carry the powerful medicine of transformation.

"Lily, please light the sage. I need to clear these. They haven't seen the light of day in many years and must be tired from so much sleep."

When the bowl of sage was lit and the smoke had begun to rise, Uncle Will took each drum and drumstick in turn, passing it through the plumes several times and laying it back on the table. He took the wing and did the same. Once this was done, he picked up the bowl and used the wing to draw some of the smoke up, passing the wing over his head. He swept smoke down his arms and the front of his body. He directed it, as best he could, around toward his back. He called Lily to him, and as she lifted her arms out to the side, he swept the smoke toward her body from top to bottom, going underneath her raised arms. He asked her to turn. He repeated these motions on her back and then asked her to lift her feet up, one at a time. He stooped down to direct the smoke toward the soles. Then he stood up, drew the tip of the wing down her upper back and gently tapped the top of each shoulder. Lily walked away.

Will paused, waiting for Jack, who had watched all this with a mixture of curiosity and amazement. He'd seen Lily pray before, but he'd never witnessed anything like this. He stepped forward, breathed in the fragrant smoke, and let it out with a sigh. He felt his lizard-skin patches tingle when the smoke was directed over them. When he felt Will's tap on his shoulders, he went back to stand next to Lily. Then, Will said some words in a language Jack couldn't understand, as he turned slowly, directing the smoke toward each of the four directions, then up to the sky and down to the earth. After this, he walked all around the room, sweeping smoke into the corners—coming back to the kitchen table, to pay special attention to the area above and around the chair where his nephew had been sitting.

He put the bowl and wing back on the table, and got the sage and tobacco from the countertop. He piled more sage on top of the still smoldering leaves, topping this with a pinch of tobacco. Another pinch of tobacco was rubbed over the surface of the drums and dropped into the bowl. Then he handed the smaller drum to Jack and said, "Follow me."

Lily held her hands behind her back and bowed her head. Will closed his eyes and began to drum. Jack picked up his beat: 1-2,3,4; 1-2,3,4; 1-2,3,4. Soon, Will began to sing. Lily accompanied him, repeating the beginning of each round of words while Will waited, and then continuing on with him as he sang the rest of the song.

Jack was deeply moved by the power in Will's voice; these songs brought an undeniable feeling of sacredness to this moment. He realized Will must be calling on Spirits to come to this place and he felt the energy of the room growing. Finally, Will quietly sang a few words, made a series of soft, rapid drumbeats, and the song was over. Will began to pray aloud.

Jack expected to hear a typical prayer that earnestly asked for help and begged for it to come quickly; but instead, Will began with words of gratitude to the Ancestors and Spirit Helpers who had come, asking to be forgiven for his long absence from their counsel. He thanked them for watching over his family, and for coming now to hear his prayers about his nephew. He thanked them for their guidance and all the understanding, peace and love that would come into his family as they watched his nephew healing. He thanked them for the blessing of having Lily and her friend come to his home on the mountain. Finally, he thanked them for their teaching that helped him live his life in a good way, all his days. His prayer finished, Will picked up his drum and sang another song. Putting his drum on the table, Will turned to hug Lily. He hugged Jack. Lily hugged Jack, too.

"Come," Will said. The three walked back out into the quickly cooling night. Will tamped down the embers, still glowing in the bowl. When he was satisfied that they were

The Greatest Enchantment

completely out, he walked to the edge of the forest and turned the bowl over to release its contents into the grass.

"Lily," Jack managed. "I'm so glad…"

Lily put a finger up to his lips, to quiet him. He reached up, held her finger there for a moment and kissed it. This seemed to surprise him as much as it did Lily. Looking into his eyes, she felt a new softness in his gaze.

Uncle Will walked back, saying, "Well, that sure felt good," and they all laughed, releasing the tension, and went back into the house—all except the Fairies, who chose to head up to their tree home and contemplate all that had taken place today.

As they flew in, they were surprised to see their space was already occupied.

"Hello," exclaimed one of three fluttering Fairies—all with wispy white hair; dressed in identical indigo tunics. "I'm Twiliter, and these are my friends, Makesmoon and Blubee."

"We're…," Runawind began.

"Oh, we know all about you. Plenty told us everything," Blubee said with an excited flutter. "He sent us here to tell you what he and the Singer have cooked-up."

"Yes," Makesmoon sighed. "It's been a long time since those two have cooked-up a plan."

"Indeed," Twiliter agreed. "Too long; but this one's bound to make up for that!" The three Fairies laughed and fluttered happily.

"And we all have a part to play," Makesmoon said, when they quieted down again. "We're here to tell you yours."

Melarose and Runawind listened with awe as the plot unfolded. Things had to move fast now. Utmost secrecy was also required, of course.

"He does see you, you know," Blubee mentioned in a most casual way.

"Who does?" Runawind asked.

"Will. He sees us all—just like Lily," Makesmoon answered, sending a tinkling laugh toward Runawind's look of surprise.

"Never mind. We'll be back tomorrow," Twiliter smiled, and the three Fairy Messengers fluttered off into the night.

The next morning, the Fairies peered out of their tree home to see everything on the mountaintop shrouded in a thick silver mist. They knew this had been sent by the Otherworld to open a doorway between the realms. A golden glow was just visible, coming from the kitchen window. Someone was up and about in the house. They stretched their mental antenna to investigate, and found it wasn't Lily.

Making their way easily through the enchanted fog, Melarose and Runawind peered into the kitchen window, where they saw Will at the sink, filling a coffee pot with water. Will looked up at them and smiled. They stared back at him with wide eyes and mouths forming a tiny 'o', till he disappeared from view. When they heard the screen door open, they flew over, and Will motioned them to come inside.

"But," Runawind could not suppress his questions. "Why didn't you let us know you could see us?"

"It's been my habit for thirty years to ignore the things I see. It would upset my wife if she heard me talking to myself in the kitchen or out in the yard. The first time it happened, she asked me why. I told her, and it upset her even more to think there were things she couldn't see."

"But," Runawind started again.

"I loved my wife. I never doubted that, or her love for me. I gave up my world to be in hers, where she would feel safe and happy."

"That was a big sacrifice," Melarose whispered.

"We both made sacrifices to be together," Will replied. "Her friends thought she was crazy to be with me; an Indian with no more ambition than to teach math at the local elementary school. Her father had made a comfortable living from his law practice, and she was his only child. He'd wanted more for her, so he was also against our relationship. It didn't help that he and my Dad had quarreled for many years, and couldn't even be in the same room. But my father-in-law was not a well man, and Josie's mother had passed away some years before. He knew that, when he was gone, she'd be alone in the world and have to fend for herself. I think he preferred having a man like me there—someone he could see truly loved her—to leaving his daughter with no one to lean on. So, he finally gave in and let us get married."

"But," Runawind's mind seemed stuck on the same key.

"I never asked him, but I think he may have also known something else. This room I'm standing in was once part of a house that belonged to my great-great grandmother. Our family was among the lucky ones who were spared going on the Trail of Tears—or facing death, if we stayed behind. But we couldn't come back to what we owned; there was a reservation carved out for us instead. That was heartbreaking, and it made many of our people sick with anger. But it was far better than nothing. We would survive. I sometimes think my father-in-law took a kind of comfort from giving my family back what had been ours—even if he could never admit that to me, or anyone else."

"Did you ever tell your wife that?" Melarose asked, fluttering down to rest on his shoulder.

"No."

"What about your sons?" Runwind wondered.

"They were always more like their mother. And since I wasn't able to train them in my ways, they never developed a deep feeling for this land. I didn't think the history of the house would mean much to them. They'd decided when they were young that they had bigger fish to fry, so I knew they would leave as soon as they could; they'd try to make their way in a different world. So, when my wife passed, I changed my will and put this house in Lily's name. She'll own it outright once I pass, too."

"Does Lily know that?" Melarose asked.

"No one does. I'll tell her when the time is right," Will said. "That's why you saw me crying those tears of joy when I heard she'd come back." Will smiled. "I trusted her connection to this place and the teaching her Grandma gave her. I was so glad to see I was right."

"So, you think she'll stay? What about Jack?" Runawind asked.

"I've seen a lot of change in Jack today. At first, he was just trying to charm me. When we took that drive around the area, I knew that no matter what he said, he was looking at everything to see if it was a place he could build something to his advantage. But then, I took him up to some holy ground on a ridge nearby. While he looked out at the mountains, I told him the story of our people. He told me some about his family—how his great-grandparents fled their own country to stay alive before the last world war began. He let me see into his heart, and he saw into mine. Something changed for him."

"And then, he came back and there was Lily, with Danny," Melarose sighed.

"Yes. I could see that, what he felt then made him realize he could never hurt her." Will smiled. "And later, I handed him the drum."

"The drum," Runawind exclaimed. "You wanted him to play the heartbeat of Mother Earth."

"It was a test, and he passed. But, I can see Lily has a choice to make here, and we have to let her make it," Will said. "You know, Josie had the voice of an angel," he continued, changing the subject. "The boys and I would play guitar and banjo, and she would play her dulcimer and sing. I swear she spoke to Spirit with her voice, just like our people do." Tears glistened in Will's eyes. "She sang for me the day before she passed. Not even her illness could take away that angel voice."

Melarose brushed some Fairy kisses on his cheek.

"Well, it's time to get the coffee going," Will said. "They'll be up soon—and from the look of that fog out there, this is going to be a big day. We'll all need a good breakfast to give us strength," he said, opening the screen door. "When you see Plenty, please tell him what we talked about. He's been very patient with me, and I do appreciate it."

"We will," the Fairies said, and flew into the silver mist.

"Hey hi hi ya, hey hi yo. The top of the world is the place to go. Hey hi hi ya, hey hi yay. I am the Keeper of the Way."

Melarose and Runawind heard Plenty singing, long before they could see him in the thick mist. They followed the sound and discovered him—hard at work, rolling bits of herbs and flowers into packets made of rhododendron leaves and securing them with strands of corn silk. The Fairies landed on top of a large toadstool nearby, and watched.

"So, you met my Messengers, did you?" Plenty asked.

"Yes, and Will said to tell you…" Runawind began.

"Praise the day," Plenty exclaimed, cutting in. "He's come to himself again, at last."

The Fairies told him all that Will had said.

"Oh, he was always a good lad," Plenty beamed. "There's none of us Elves that can ever figure why humans choose to love who they do. But love each other, they did—that I could easily see. I'm glad that Lily coming home and telling her story let him remember who he was before."

'We didn't tell him the plan, of course, but he seems to know something important is going to happen today."

"He will have dreamt it, too," Plenty said.

"But how are we going to get everyone back up here?" Melarose asked.

"The Messengers will even now be with the ones they need to inspire," Plenty laughed. "We have our own ways of magic here. You'll see—it will all happen easily enough. Now get on back to the house. You two need to be there when Grandma Rainmaker arrives and help Lily bring her here, to get these packets I prepared."

"Okay," Runawind said.

They were only half-way back when they heard a phone ringing in the house and Lily's voice saying 'hello' to her Grandmother. By the time they got there, Lily was on the porch, staring into the mist that had begun to lift in some places—one of which, oddly enough, was the road down the mountain.

"Lily," Melarose said aloud, coming to light on her shoulder. "Runawind and I have removed the telepathic charm."

"Why?" Lily asked.

"You don't need it now. And, we found out today that your Uncle Will can see and hear us, too," Melarose confided.

"He can?"

"Apparently, he always could," Runawind added. "But he hid it for his wife's sake, and just got used to ignoring it."

"That part makes sense." Lily sighed. She had loved her Aunt Josie, but remembered being scolded by her several times for indulging in silly fantasies. "I need to pick up Grandma. For some reason she really wants to come over today, even with this dense fog, and rain in the forecast."

"We'll come with you," Melrose offered.

"This fog is strange," Lily said to her Grandmother on the ride back to Will's house. "The only place it seems to be clear enough to see is on this road."

"Do you remember what I told you about fog and the Otherworld?" Grandma asked.

"Are you saying...," Lily began.

"You said your Uncle Will prayed last night. That made my heart so glad," Grandma said. "You weren't even born when he married, so you can't remember how deeply he was involved in his spiritual work. But then, all that changed," Grandma sighed. "It took me many years to see that it was all for the best."

"For the best?"

"There is a time for things, Lily, and we don't always know what it is, or why people walk off the path we envision for them."

"You mean he was taking his own true path, no matter how it looked then?"

"Oh, yes. And there was a lot of happiness on that road, no matter what my husband and I thought. He deserved that happiness, and in time, it brought all of us a great treasure we could not have foreseen."

"What treasure?"

"I think I'll let you find out about that, just the way I did." Grandma smiled.

Melarose flew to Grandma's ear and whispered something to her.

"You can tell Plenty I'll be right along, once I've had some of my son's wonderful eggs and grits," she laughed. "And another cup of coffee to wash down this cake I brought him."

"You're going to see Plenty?" Lily was surprised at another unusual turn of events.

"And you're coming with me," Grandma answered. "Oh, good, we're here. Take the cake and run on in. Tell your Uncle to start cooking."

Lily did as she was told. Grandma got out of the car with Melarose and Runawind. "Go on now. You, too," she said, laughing and shooing them away with her hand. She closed the car door and stood alone in the silver mist. "My dearest love, the day has come," she whispered to the sky. "Our son, Will Singing Bear, has come back to us." Closing her eyes, she felt a soft, moist breeze caress her cheeks. She blew a kiss toward the sky, turned, and made her way to the house.

The fog was beginning to lift in the area around Uncle Will's house. Melarose and Runawind became anxious to lead Grandma Rainmaker and Lily to Plenty. Will saw them fluttering at the kitchen door, turned to his mother and said, "It's time."

Grandma Rainmaker nodded, got up, and put on her prayer shawl. She handed another to Lily, who quickly put it around her shoulders, and they both went outside. Shawls were used for ceremony, so Lily knew something important was going to be happening today. She knew better than to question her Grandmother about it, too, and trusted she could just follow along. They hadn't walked very far when they heard Plenty's song, and soon, they saw the Elf, dancing in circles around a small pile of wrapped packets.

"Hey hi hi ya, hey hi yay. Magic is afoot today. Hey hi hi ya, hey hi yo. Magic with them all will go. Magic is afoot today. Hey hi hi ya, hey hi yay," Plenty sang. Coming to a stop, he flashed a big smile at the two women. "Welcome," he said, with a deep bow. He straightened up and pointed at the pile of neatly tied leaves. "Those are for you, and there's one for everyone who will come into the woods with me. Please choose a bundle and put it somewhere on yourself, tucked down safe—it is your magical protection that you must carry. Divide the rest between you, and find a way to get them into the pockets of the others."

Grandma had a pinch of tobacco that she sprinkled on the ground in front of the little pile. "Thank you, Plenty," she said, stooping low to retrieve her bundle. Lily came forward and repeated her Grandmother's gesture. When Lily had secured hers in her jeans pocket, she picked up the remaining bundles, and handed two to Grandma Rainmaker.

"I'll be here waiting," Plenty said. He commenced to sing and dance again, and the two women started back to the house. Melarose and Runawind were riding Lily's shoulder to stay in the orb of her protection in case the Shadow waited nearby. They didn't see it, but they knew the fog might hide its whereabouts. And they also knew it might already be attached to the young man who must, even now, be waiting in the kitchen.

Because of the number of bundles they had, Lily expected to see her mother's white car arrive. She was surprised when, instead, she saw Danny's black pick-up truck parked near the back steps. When they walked into the house, four men were seated around the kitchen table.

"I picked Billy up," Danny said by way of greeting. Grandma smiled and offered her thanks.

Billy was slouched in his chair, head down, looking at no one. "Why am I here?" he muttered to no one in particular.

"Oh, you'll see," Grandma said as gently as she could, leaning over to embrace him, and slipping a bundle in his pants pocket as he tried to shrug her off.

"The fog is lifting, so we'll be able to see the path," Lily said.

She went first to Jack, smiled up at him, and deposited a bundle in the pocket of his denim jacket, while saying, "The woods are very special in this kind of weather. I believe we're all going for a walk—want to come?"

He nodded, so she left him, and went to deliver her last bundle.

"Danny, it's good to see you again," she said, giving him a quick hug and putting the bundle in his hand. He knew what to do with it. So did Will, who quietly received his from his mother.

Sage was already piled high in the bowl on the table. Will struck a match and lit it, saying a prayer. He used the birdwing fan to brush the smoke around the room and over everyone in it, including himself. He, Lily, and his mother sang a song.

"We are so grateful for this day," Will said, when they finished.

The Greatest Enchantment

"And all the beauty that we'll find on our way," his mother added.

"Come on—let's go to the woods," Will said, and followed his mother out the door. Billy grudgingly got up, walking ahead of Jack, whose face held a bemused look. Lily and Danny brought up the rear; with Melarose and Runawind, still sitting on Lily's shoulder.

When they got outside, Melarose spotted the three Fairy Messengers. "Runawind, look," she whispered.

The three Fairies held small gossamer bags, and flew above the slowly moving group, sprinkling Fairy Dust on them, and softly singing in the Fairy Tongue. The enchantment had begun.

For some in the group, it was like a dream; for others, just another level of reality manifesting, when they encountered the Elf, singing and dancing in a circle. For once, Billy was standing up straight; all his attention focused on the little man with the long black beard. Jack was laughing with delight at this peculiar sight. Lily heard Danny sigh with satisfaction.

When the Elf became silent, Grandma Rainmaker took the lead, and they followed Plenty onto a barely visible path into the woods. The three Fairy Messengers fluttered quickly up to Melarose and Runawind, giving them each a gossamer bag of Fairy Dust to tie around their waist. Blowing kisses, they waved goodbye, and flew back toward the house.

It seemed to Lily that the trees whispered to them as they walked along. The tops of the tallest were shrouded by the mist. "It's so beautiful," she thought, walking along with Jack ahead of her, and Danny following behind. Jack seemed eager as an innocent boy in wonderland.

All at once, a deep, gravelly voice began singing. Like a loud drumbeat, it reverberated off the tree trunks. "It's the Singer of the Wood," Melarose whispered in Lily's ear. The air around her felt full; like velvet drapes, caressing her skin.

Plenty had stopped, and began directing them all into forming a semi-circle at the edge of gnarled roots, below a mighty oak. The Singer began to arise. They all watched, transfixed and mesmerized by the glinting green eyes. The song became even louder. The words entered their consciousness—filling their brain, running in their blood, crackling along their nerve pathways.

"Hey hi hi ya, hey hi yo. To the mountain you must go. He hi hi ya, hey hi yay. Only love can lead the way. Only love can lead the way. Hey hi hi ya, hey hi yay." Soon, they were singing this song along with the mysterious creature who, despite having no visible mouth, seemed to be smiling.

Their singing continued on, until a small concentrated beam of white light appeared in the center of the oak's massive trunk. It grew and grew, taking on a golden glow. When the light suddenly vanished, they saw it had created a large oval doorway that opened into a brightly lit garden. Plenty walked through and motioned for them to follow. With Grandma Rainmaker in the lead, they passed through the portal doorway, and into the unknown.

Chapter 7

ONLY LOVE

Grandma and Uncle Will walked ahead and entered a circle of paved stones in the midst of the brilliant emerald-green grass. There they stood, facing a stone path that led toward a mountain; shimmering with green, white, and gold light. Another path of brick on the left of the circle led toward the banks of a sparkling sapphire-blue river. Everything here was vivid and welcoming. Even the air seemed to twinkle, and each sweet breath bestowed a feeling of well-being.

Billy and Jack had stopped just inside the portal doorway and seemed unable to go on. Lily looked back and stopped, too, wondering what to do about this. Danny gave her cheek a thoughtful caress, and when he saw her smile, he went on to join the others in the circle.

"Is this the Otherworld?" Lily asked her Fairy Friends.

Melarose giggled. "Not THE Otherworld, but it's another world, to be sure," she said. "Please wait here. There's something for you to see."

Runawind flew off Lily's shoulder and opened his gossamer pouch. He headed for Jack. Melarose opened hers and flew to Billy. They each took a pinch of sparkling Fairy Dust and blew a tiny bit over the heart area of the humans, saying in unison, "What stops you from feeling love?"

Jack said, "It will hurt too much when it's gone."

Billy said, "I know that no one cares about me."

After blowing another bit of Fairy Dust, the Fairies asked, "What stops you from giving love?"

Jack said, "It hurts when they don't love me back."

"I know they will leave me," Billy replied.

Lily's eyes welled with tears. She wanted to reach out and hold them both, but she felt rooted to the spot.

Melarose and Runawind nodded at each other, flew back to her, and began to sprinkle some Fairy Dust over her head. "Who must you love most of all?"

She was surprised to hear herself say, "First, and most of all, I must love myself."

"Why is that true?"

"When I love myself, I accept the love of Creator, who made me exactly as I am."

"And why is this important?"

"Because when I am full of love, I can truly love and care for all creatures and all things."

When she finished saying this, she realized that Jack and Billy had been listening to her, too. She could tell that they wanted to argue with her, and that their minds were putting forth reasons why what she'd said was wrong.

The Fairies sprinkled another bit of Fairy Dust over her head and asked, "What does love of Self feel like?"

She took a deep breath, closed her eyes and opened herself to receive and feel the love of Creator pouring into her. Every cell of her body hummed with warm energy; her mind repeated the words, "only love." She knew that, for those who could see it, she was radiating pink, green and gold light. "It feels like total joy," she answered, and heard the Fairies giggling with happiness.

She opened her eyes, walked to Jack and Billy and reached out to lightly touch their hearts with her fingertips. Looking from one to the other, she said, "I can't do this for you—no one can. It's up to you whether you choose joy or hold onto your suffering. But I can tell you what I know. There is no one alive that hasn't felt pain. There is no one alive that hasn't had moments of self-doubt. There is no one, and no group of people, that has ever escaped the negative judgment and ill-will of others. And despite all this, there is no one that isn't loved, and loved completely, by Creator. When you are ready, you will see this is true. Then, you will have a different answer to those questions; then, you will have a different life." Lily smiled, dropped her hands, and went to join the others in the circle.

"Well done, dear girl," she heard a familiar voice say. Looking to her right, she saw Incantaro, flying alongside. She remembered his words to her in the car. It was only a few days ago, but it felt like a lifetime. "Time is a funny thing, even in your world," Incantaro smiled. "And now is the time of choosing," he said, and they entered the circle.

A part of Lily wanted to look back and see what was happening with Billy and Jack. But the mountain ahead was so beautiful. She knew that each person was here for their own experience; she couldn't miss hers by worrying about them now.

"Very good," Incantaro said. "Humans often mistake a healthy self-interest for selfishness, when truly it is best for everyone when we take good care of ourselves. Think of how relieved your mother will be if Billy chooses to do that."

She saw that this was true. "Why isn't my mother here?" she asked.

"She isn't ready, Lily," Incantaro said. "Remember how you felt, just before you left home? Your mother feels even more hopeless than you did. She built a wall around her heart that she thought would protect her from the unkind behavior of others, and her own feelings of disappointment and despair. But once those walls are built, they stop even those who love us from getting close. Your mother paces behind that wall. She can't see it, and she can't find a way out."

"That's so sad," Lily said.

"Yes, it is—but in time you will see the power that witnessing a change in others will have for her. Sometimes people need to see a miracle to believe one can happen for them."

Lily accepted this, and wondered what kind of things her Grandmother, Uncle Will and Danny were experiencing.

"They have their own Guides, who are with them now. It is an important day for all of you," Incantaro explained.

So...Incantaro was here just for her, she thought; what an honor that was.

"I'm one of the Guides who have been with you since you were born, dear girl," Incantaro said. "Now it is time for you to know this, and to get to know me well. You may meet all your Guides someday. And, again I say, that you may call on me, whenever there is need."

She wondered how she got to have a Fairy Wizard as a guide.

"You have spent several lives as a Fairy yourself," Incantaro replied. "Those who can see us and hear our call have often been Fairies themselves, for the human is not normally so attuned."

Then, it was not by accident that Melarose and Runawind came to Jack's home, she thought, and that I was living next door. This idea provoked a sparkling Wizard laugh. "There is not one moment that isn't part of a larger plan—one agreed upon by all," he said when his mirth was done. "The sooner you understand this, the easier all experiences will be. You will have less of a need to know; instead, you will be able to watch life unfurl, in the same way a beautiful rose opens to the sun."

"Why don't we already see life that way?"

"There was a time when humans lived close to the earth and knew her bounty and her blessing. But, unlike other creatures and kingdoms in your world, the humans became dissatisfied, and looked for ways to improve things. They turned their focus from following and enjoying the cycles and rhythms, and nurtured a desire to take the lead. They forgot their own agreements with all the kingdoms, seeking to overpower nature and bend it to their will. It really is as simple as that."

"But only love can truly lead the way?"

"Only love," Incantaro said. "And when it does, miracles happen. Now, you must join the others and go to the mountain."

"What about Billy and Jack?"

"They are here now, behind you in this circle. When they're ready, they'll take a dip in the beautiful lake where the refreshing sapphire waters will wash away many layers of the emotional decisions that have stopped their progress. But for now, dear girl, don't look back. Remember the perfection of the agreements made by all, and let this time unfurl. I promise you will all be together when it's time to return to your world."

She smiled at the Wizard, and took a step forward onto the path. From that point, her thinking mind remembered nothing more. She knew only that, with that first step toward the shimmering mountain, her feelings of happiness had increased—and when she found herself standing once again in the semi-circle in front of the massive oak tree, she felt a peace within her that was greater than she had ever felt before.

The Singer of the Woods was still there, too. The Singer rose higher, and leaned forward—glittering green eyes peering at each of the humans in turn. "We may close the doorway," the Singer told Plenty. The Elf began a clockwise dance around the oak tree, as the Singer's voice rose in another powerful song. "Hi hi hi ya, hi ya hey. Love has brought the Golden Day. Now Love leads you on your way. Hi hi hi ya, hi ya hey."

The song went on and on, until Lily perceived that they were all following Plenty back out of the woods and into Uncle Will's yard. Sunlight streamed down through thin layers of silver mist, floating high above. Lily felt Melarose and Runawind return to her shoulder. Each planted a Fairy Kiss on her cheek.

"Soon, all will seem to wake," Melarose whispered in her ear. "They will see a cloudless sky with an early afternoon sun, shining bright. It will seem to everyone as though you are all out here to greet Danny and Billy, arriving at Will's house for lunch."

"But..." Lily began.

"It will be different than before," Runawind said.

"Will they..."

"Only three others will remember that an enchantment took place," Runawind giggled.

"And the Shadow?"

"Billy isn't weak anymore," Melarose said. "The Shadow's gone."

"Where did it go?"

"They don't go anywhere, because they don't exist in the way you imagine," Runawind explained. "They come into being where there are many dark thoughts and feelings. Then they look for a host to feed them a constant energy supply. If they manage to latch on, it can be impossible to overcome them. And it isn't wise to combat them directly, either, because that can backfire."

"Why?"

"Because any form of struggle or attack is darkness. This is something humans, and even some elementals, don't seem to understand. Only the very wise, firmly rooted in their inner light, can successfully counter a negative force without becoming part of the darkness they hope to defeat."

"So, now Billy is no longer full of that darkness and the Shadow couldn't attach," Lily offered. "And there was nothing in the circle of love we were in when we returned from the portal to create it. It's as simple as that?" Fairy giggles confirmed that she was right.

"I think it's time," Melarose said to Runawind. They flew above the humans, sprinkling Fairy Dust over them with a dramatic flourish. Snapping their Fairy Fingers three times, they said together, "It is done."

"Danny—thanks for picking up our boy, here," Will said, walking towards him. Billy was standing on the other side of Danny's truck, smiling.

"Sure, any time, Will." Danny shook Will's hand. "It gave us a chance to talk about a wood-working class I'm teaching next month. I think he's interested."

"That so?" Will smiled, as Billy came around the truck. He gave him a sideways shoulder hug.

"Yes," Billy replied. "I want to learn how to make furniture, too, one day."

"Well, that's great. Come on in now everyone." Will gestured toward the house. "That pork roast Lily made has been resting just long enough."

"Pork roast I made?" Lily whispered, and heard the Fairies giggling.

"The best one ever," Runawind said.

"But—how?"

"There were lots of helpers today, Lily," Melarose answered. "What happened here was important—and to more kingdoms than you can imagine."

"She'll see," the ever-impatient Runawind told Melarose. "Let's get inside."

Will's kitchen was filled with the wonderful aromas of food and wild flowers. Everyone busied themselves, helping get the meal onto the big table in the dining room. Those who remembered something of the day's enchantment gave each other special glances and smiles. Lily had never seen her Grandmother this happy—or anyone else for that matter. Even Jack seemed perfectly relaxed and carefree.

Runawind had been right. It was the best pork roast ever. Everyone had seconds; some even had third helpings of this special feast. They were all so busy savoring their meal that conversation didn't begin until the last dinner plate was off the table and dessert was ready to be served.

With her authority as cutter of the chocolate layer cake, Grandma began. "So, Jack—what do you think of this part of the world?"

Jack sighed. "I haven't felt as good as I do here in a long time," he admitted. "The waterfall Lily took me to, the lookouts Will showed me on our drive yesterday, and the walk we took into the woods this morning—honestly? It's like heaven."

Grandma gave him a big grin as a reward, and passed him a piece of cake. "How long do you expect to stay? I hear you have a business down south."

Jack looked over at Lily. "I haven't thought about it. I'd like to experience more of this place; but I guess that depends on how Will and Lily feel about it, too."

"Stay as long as you like," Will said, accepting his slice of cake. Lily just smiled.

"That's very generous of you, Will," Jack said. "I have a few ideas I'd like to toss around with you—maybe later today."

Lily's heart skipped a beat. Was he going to propose some real estate deal?

"Don't be too sure," Melarose whispered. "Just let his words pass, and we'll find out later."

After this, the conversation became more general and humor prevailed. Lily was overjoyed to see Billy joining in. She also wished she could have some time with Danny alone, to find out how much he remembered of the experience they'd had. As if in reply to her thought, Danny said he should be on his way. Jack offered to drive Billy back to town so he could stay on and visit for a while, and Billy accepted.

When Danny's goodbyes had been said, Lily got up to see him to his truck.

"Walk with me?" Danny asked when they were outside.

"You read my mind."

They set off on the path they had taken earlier; but Danny chose to follow a branch that led downhill. Soon, Lily heard the soft sounds of a gurgling creek, and they came upon a clearing. Smooth rocks near the water's edge looked like a perfect place to sit. Sitting together comfortably on the largest rock, they stared at the dappled sunlight on the water, listening to bees, buzzing over the heads of wild flowers. So far, neither of them had said a word. Danny reached over and took her hand.

"I did," he said softly.

"You did what?" she asked.

"Read your mind," he replied. "For some reason, it always seemed like I could."

"And what am I thinking now?"

"You want to know about today; if I remember anything about it."

"Yes. That's true."

"Well," he said, entwining his fingers with hers. "I don't really remember anything after we started toward the mountain. Before that, my Guide was talking with me. And before that, there was the most amazing creature—it looked like a woman made of roots, with green cat's eyes. She sang powerful songs."

"I remember the same. And there was a kind of doorway on the tree," she said.

The Greatest Enchantment

"Yes," Danny replied. "And I remember some things my Guide told me, and some things I agreed to do."

"Can you tell me?" Lily asked.

"Yes—and I will. But there's one I need to show you," he said. And with that, he leaned over, turned her face to his, and kissed her. Though his lips were gentle, a power in their touch joined their hearts. Danny reluctantly ended the kiss, smiled, and said, "You had to know, without a doubt, how I feel about you. Now, it will be easier for you to make up your mind."

Surprised, Lily was tempted to act as if she didn't know what he meant. But it made sense that he had observed her attraction to Jack; he was saying he would be patient. "Thank you, Danny," she whispered. "That means a lot to me."

They stood up and he took her in his arms. It was then she realized that she hadn't fully returned from the enchantment. The comfort of his embrace was just what she needed to bring her back to earth in the nicest possible way. He took her hand, and they began the walk back to the house. When they reached the yard, after another soft kiss on her forehead, Danny got into his truck and drove away.

Lily heard the screen door open and close. When she turned, she saw Uncle Will coming down the steps. He asked her to walk around to the front of the house with him.

"Danny offered to take it, you know," Will said, when they were both seated on white rocking chairs on the front porch.

"What do you mean?"

"He offered to take the Shadow to save Billy, if that was the only way," Will said. "He felt he was strong enough to defeat it. And he might have been, too. But I'm glad we'll never have to know."

"How did you hear that?"

"Mom told me, when I called to tell her you were back."

Lily thought about what Incantaro had said about the agreements they had all made.

"Do you think I should be there when Jack talks to you later?"

"I think it's important that you're there, Lily. But now," Will said. "We need to stay clear of the kitchen and let your Grandma do her work."

"Shouldn't I be helping?"

"Not with this kind of work. Have you noticed your little friends aren't with you?"

"No," Lily laughed. "Are they still in the house?"

"They're helping your Grandma do her work with Jack and Billy. All things weren't settled during the journey we took earlier," he said. "We'll sit out here till we get the all-clear. I'll tell you what happened for me today, and you can tell me your experience ... if you want to." Sighing with contentment, he looked out at the mountain view before him. "It sure is a beautiful day."

"It sure is," Lily agreed.

Jack and Billy started to get up from the dining table, but Grandma Rainmaker asked them to stay. She reached into her skirt pocket and brought out a red velvet bag—from it, she pulled a shiny black seed. It was oval-shaped; the size of her thumbnail. As she did this, the Fairies flew over to Jack and Billy, and sprinkled a pinch of Fairy Dust on them, whispering words that put them back into a light trance. Grandma waited till their faces took on an open, dreamy look.

"You see this seed?" she asked them, placing it on the table between them. "It has special power. The person who eats this seed will always be able to increase all he has. Unfortunately, I only have one. I know it's not for me. It has to be for one of you."

Billy and Jack looked down at the shiny seed.

"Who do you think should have it?" she asked.

Some moments passed while Jack and Billy looked across the table at each other.

"I don't have much, so there's nothing for me to increase," Billy finally said. "Give the seed to Jack."

Grandma reached out to take the seed and do as Billy suggested, but Jack stopped her.

"No. That's not true Billy. Yes, I have a lot of money and property. But you have a wonderful family who love and support you—and there's Danny, who's going to teach you how to do something you'll enjoy. All that will increase if you take the seed," Jack said, and turned to look at Grandmother. "He should have it."

Grandmother Rainmaker's smile was so bright that, if it were nighttime, it would have lit the whole room. "Well, since your wishes are clear, there's only one thing to do now." She opened the velvet bag again, and took out a small, gold knife with a thin, razor-sharp blade. Carefully, she cut the seed into two perfect halves. "Take one half and eat it. Never forget the friendship and respect you have shown each other through your unselfish words. Because of this, all that is good in your lives—and more important, all that is good in yourselves—will continue to increase."

When they had followed her directions, Melarose and Runawind snapped their Fairy Fingers three times and said, "It is done." Then they flew off to the screen door at the front of the house, to let Will and Lily know the test was over.

"Look at the time," Grandma said, as Jack and Billy came back into reality. "I think I need a nap. Would you mind driving me to my house, Jack?"

Before he could answer, Will and Lily entered the kitchen. "That's okay Momma," Will said. "I'll take you. Why don't you young folks go visit the Indian Village? I don't believe Jack has seen that."

"Oconaluftee?" Lily asked. Uncle Will nodded. "Would you like that, Jack?"

"Sure," Jack replied. "Let me go splash some water on my face. I'll be with you in a minute."

"He's a good man," Grandma said, when Jack had left the room. "You go freshen up, too, Lily. It's already been a long day."

"A golden day," Lily said, returning Grandma's smile and getting a big, comforting bear-hug.

"Now you," Grandma said to Billy, who went willingly into her arms. "I'm so proud of you. Tell your Momma I want to see you both soon."

Billy nodded, and walked outside with Grandma, to see her off. Melarose and Runawind followed Lily.

When they were in her room and the door was closed, the Fairies told Lily what had happened in the kitchen with Jack and Billy. Lily sat down on her bed and started to cry.

"What's wrong?" Melarose asked. "You should be happy to hear this."

"I am—but Danny kissed me—and now Jack is proving to be a better man than I had thought. What am I going to do?"

"Do you have to do anything?" Melarose asked.

"I have to make a choice."

"But not now," Runawind said.

"Not today," Melarose agreed. "There is still time for hearts to be revealed, and then the way will become clear."

"When we came here, I thought all Jack would do was look for land to ruin with big houses. I thought he would be a lizard again in no time. I had no real faith in him," Lily admitted. "And I never thought Danny would be waiting for me all these years. I always pictured him with a wife and children, living a happy life."

"And so now you see that, no matter what we may think, we don't always know. That's a good reason to give things more time, isn't it?" Melarose told her.

"No one is forcing your decision," Runawind added.

"Stay focused in the present time. Keep observing, and allow your own true feelings to surface." Melarose suggested.

"You're right," Lily said. Getting up, she went into the bathroom and picked up the acorn. She put it in her pocket for good luck. Then she washed her face, brushed her hair and put on pale-pink lipstick. She took a moment to appraise her reflection in the mirror. "I'm ready," she said.

Melarose and Runawind chose to stay behind. Once they were outside, they quickly flew off to find Plenty. They couldn't wait to tell him what had happened since they returned to the house. But when they finally found him, he was lying between two rows of sunflowers, enjoying what appeared to be a deep, deep sleep. The Fairies couldn't help giggling as each of Plenty's exhales produced a high-pitched whistle. Soon, this sound reminded them of how tired they were, too.

The Greatest Enchantment

Up to their little tree snug they flew, expecting nothing more than a quiet nap.

Instead, they found they had a visitor. Incantaro welcomed them into their own little home-away-from-home, and said, "I'm pleased and proud of the way you both have handled your assignment so far. I know how hard it is to be in this human world for so long; how much energy it requires. I know how much you must long to be back on our mountain; in Fairy Time, flying with your friends. And I will leave you soon, to take your rest." He smiled. "But first, I have important information to impart."

As the Fairies listened, their eyes grew wide, and their fluttering wings sent out sparks of light from all the excitement caused by the Wizard's words.

"And now, enjoy your nap," Incantaro concluded. "You'll have need of even more energy as this day progresses." And with a wink, the Wizard was gone.

Though the Fairies wondered how they could rest after hearing what Incantaro had to say, they soon fell into a sound, dreamless sleep.

Meanwhile, in the yard below, Jack gave Billy the keys to the SUV, saying, "You know the way." Billy seemed pleased.

On the ride to the Indian Village, they all enjoyed a companionable silence. Once they were at the visitor's office, Lily asked if Uncle Will's friend Charlie was there. Charlie had the look of a big, friendly bear. He was also knowledgeable about Cherokee history; how they used the land, and built their homes. He would make a great tour guide for Jack.

When Charlie came out to greet them, Lily introduced Jack, but decided to let them all go off on the tour without her. She needed to see if she could find some people she knew, who might still be working here. Word must have gotten around that she was back, and she didn't want to seem unfriendly now. And even more than that, she felt the need for some time to be on her own, without Jack or Danny nearby.

She wandered over to the crafts area and found several women working there who were mothers of high school friends;

and a couple of her old classmates, too. They said nothing about her sudden departure years ago, but were full of questions about life in Florida. Lily did her best to be upbeat about her life down there, and vague about how long she would be staying in town.

After a little while, she said she'd let them get back to what they were doing, and went to get a bottle of water and sit by herself in the shade. She was going to try focusing on the present, as Melarose had suggested. She found it was more difficult than she'd imagined—her mind kept drifting back to her walk with Danny, or the way Jack had kissed her fingers. She tried to notice what kind of feelings came with each of those memories.

"Lily?" she heard Momma's voice say through her reveries. She got up to give her a hug.

"Momma—what are you doing here?"

"I could ask the same," her mother's voice was tinged with the slight sarcasm Lily knew so well. Now that Lily understood where that attitude came from, she couldn't take it personally anymore.

"Jack and I drove Billy back into town. Will thought Jack might like to take the tour," Lily said, closely watching her mother's face. She hadn't had an enchantment. How would she take this news?

"Billy is with him?"

"Yes. They seem to be getting along really well. I just needed some time for myself, and to catch up with some old friends who work here."

"I see," Rose said, but it didn't sound as though she really did. "Well, I only worked a half-day. I decided to come up here and find out if anyone had something they wanted me to put in the store."

"I've already been over to the crafts area, but I'll come with you, if you like?"

Her mother studied her for a moment. "You look a little tired," she said. "Just rest there. I'll see you again on my way out."

"Thanks, Momma, I do feel a little tired today," she admitted, giving her surprised mother another hug. "See you later."

She watched her mother walk away, picturing her as a young woman like herself—full of questions, hopes, and fears. She thought it must be hard for Momma to be alone now, with worries about both of her children. Rose would surely meet up with Jack and Billy when their tour got to the craft area. Part of Lily wished she could be there to witness her mother's reaction to the change in her son. But for now, she was content to be alone again, with her own thoughts.

The next thing she knew, Jack was standing in front of her.
"Are you all right?" he asked.
"Fine. Wow—I must have been daydreaming."
"Day-tripping is more like it—you were really out there. I said 'hello' about three times," he laughed.
"I think I'm just tired. I hope we can have a quiet evening, and I can get to bed early."
"That sounds good to me, too. By the way, Billy and your Mom took-off. She had him loaded down with baskets and things. They said to tell you goodbye."
"How did Momma seem?"
"Okay—maybe a little uncertain. Billy's doing so much better," he said. "I think she wanted to be happy, but she just wasn't sure if what she was seeing was real."
Lily nodded, stood up and started to walk with Jack to the parking area. "I can understand that."
"Should we pick up a pizza or something? No one will have to cook," Jack suggested.
"That's a great idea; maybe some stuff for a salad, too."
"Do you want to call Will, so he knows the plan?"
"Sure." There Jack was, being kind and considerate again, Lily thought. Billy wasn't the only one who seemed to have changed a lot. She dialed Will's number, and when there was no answer, left a message.
"There's something important I want to talk to Will about this evening after dinner. I hope you'll be there, too—but I'll understand if you're too tired," Jack said, getting into the car and starting the engine.

Lily got in and closed her door. "Sure. I'll be there. I'd like to hear it." She was really curious, even though she couldn't know if she was going to like what he had to say. Apparently, he didn't intend to give her any clues about it now, so she'd just have to wait. But there was one thing she was far too curious to wait for.

"Jack," she said. "Do you remember anything about what happened in the woods today? Or back when we were up on Grandfather Mountain?"

"Not very much about today, but I can tell something went on—not just a walk in the woods before lunch. Am I right?"

"Yes, you are."

"And as for Grandfather Mountain, well, I hate to have to say this, but a few patches have come back on my feet and legs. And yes, I do remember the Wizard and what he said. Weren't there two Fairies who helped us get there?"

"Yes, but you don't see them or hear them now. They've been with us the whole way."

"Really? Are they in the car now?"

"No. They decided to stay back at the house. There's an Elf they wanted to talk to about what happened today."

"An Elf?" Jack laughed. "The only one I ever heard of was in a fairy tale; a nasty one, called Rumpelstiltskin."

"Plenty is not nasty at all. He's been with Will's family for ages."

"Honestly, Lily, I never thought I'd ever be in a serious conversation about Elves and Fairies." Jack laughed again. "But I'm even more surprised that I wish I could see them now. I'd like to thank them."

"Maybe that will happen. Stay open to the idea. And I'll tell them what you said."

Jack reached out and put his hand over hers. "I know I'll never be able to thank you enough. But I'm going to try."

Lily took a deep breath, hoping she could keep herself from crying again, and that the tear that was already rolling down her cheek hadn't been seen.

"Now," he put his hand back on the steering wheel. "Tell me how to get to the pizza place you like best."

Jack and Lily were surprised to find no one home when they got back. Lily noticed there was also no sign of Fairies, or the Elf.

"I'll pop the pizza in the oven to keep it warm," Jack said. Lily put the salad things in the refrigerator. She had just closed the door, when she heard Uncle Will's truck, coming up the drive.

"How was the tour?" he asked, coming through the door.

"Great," Jack replied. "Charlie took us around. I learned a lot. And we ran into Rose at the crafts exhibit."

"How was she?" Will asked.

"A little confused, but okay," Jack said and laughed.

"We picked up a pizza, Uncle Will. And I'll make a salad," Lily offered.

"That sounds great. But do we have time for a rest first?" he asked, and laughed. "Mom had lots of instructions for me—plans for circles and ceremonies, now that I'm back in the fold. I need a little down-time to absorb it all."

"A rest sounds good to me, too," Jack said.

"I think we could all use that," Lily agreed.

And so they parted ways, saying they'd meet back at the kitchen, at sunset.

Chapter 8

THE HEART'S CHOICE

Sunset was only a lingering memory in the sky when Lily jerked awake. She hadn't meant to fall asleep, but she now discovered she'd spent the past few hours in her dreams. She remembered them being full of whirling activity, strange sights and sounds; she'd be there still, if the crows hadn't started calling. Jumping out of bed, she wondered if the others were awake and waiting for her in the kitchen.

In the bathroom, the cold water she splashed on her face felt wonderful and helped her shake the dream images from her mind. The air seemed a bit cooler, so she pulled on a sweater before heading downstairs. In the hallway, she saw light coming from the kitchen. As she drew closer, she heard a low voice, having a one-way conversation.

"Yes, I know I should have told you, but it came up suddenly—I just felt I had to get away," she heard Jack saying. Apparently the person on the other end of the phone wasn't at all happy about Jack's long disappearance. "I knew you could take care of things," Jack continued. "I wasn't worried at all ... yes, okay, I know you're right and I'm sorry." There was another pause. Lily wished he had been on speaker so she could hear the other person's replies. "No, I'm not sure exactly when I'll be back, but I promise I'll keep in touch with you. Yes, I'll check-in every day. Thanks. Bye." She heard Jack let out a deep sigh, and it seemed the conversation must have ended. She waited a minute more outside the door to be sure, and then she walked into the kitchen.

The Greatest Enchantment

"Hi," she said to Jack's back. He was looking out the screen door, and turned around when he heard her greeting.

"Hi." He smiled. "We must have all been exhausted. I woke up when I heard some birds carrying on."

"The crows," she said. "Calling their family home for the night, or being our alarm clock—maybe both." She laughed, and went to pour herself a glass of water. "Want some?"

"Sure. Thanks. I just got off the phone with my partner. He hasn't heard from me since this whole thing began. I figured it was time for me to check-in and field the difficult questions."

"Oh. Was that hard?"

"Not too bad. But apparently someone saw us driving away in my Hummer," he said. "That's been the big news at the beach parties lately—so, again, you saved my neck."

"I did?"

"It's easy for people to imagine me taking a woman away and keeping it quiet," he shrugged. "I'm sorry if that gives you a hard time in any way."

Lily laughed. "I don't think my reputation means much to your friends. And who else would care?"

"The people you work for?"

"Oh." It seemed so long ago now, she'd completely forgotten about her employers. "I guess I should check in there soon, too." She handed him the glass of water. "Let's get that pizza back in the oven. I'm starved."

"Me, too."

"And me," Will said, coming into the room. "Did you two have crazy dreams, or was it just me?" Jack and Lily both nodded. "Not surprising. It's sure been an interesting day, don't you think?"

"I told Lily I know something happened before lunch; something more than I can remember," Jack said.

"If I told you that you were on a Spirit Journey today, what would you say?" Will asked him.

Jack sighed. "I'd say it's time to tell you the truth about why Lily and I came up to North Carolina together."

"I'm all ears," Will replied.

And so, while the pizza warmed and Lily made the salad, she listened to Jack tell the whole story of his enchantment, how Lily agreed to help him, and what he remembered of that night on Grandfather Mountain; but also, he talked about how grateful he was; how much had happened in the two days since he'd been up here on the mountain; and how he now felt changed again, but in a better way this time.

When he was done, Will reached over and gave him a friendly clap on the shoulder. "You sure came to the right place," Will said and laughed, putting them all at ease. "Thanks for being honest with me, Jack. I know that took a lot of courage. But there are no walls between us now, and we can be easy with each other—more than before. I'm really glad."

"I am, too," Jack said.

Lily put the salad bowl down and handed Jack plates and silverware to distribute. Will got the pizza out of the oven and they all sat down at the kitchen table.

"Okay," Will said. "We'll have dinner—then you can tell us what's been on your mind."

Melarose and Runawind had been woken by the crow calls, too. They flew down to watch Plenty, singing and dancing to another of his songs. When he finished, they told him what had transpired since they had entered Will's house.

The Elf laughed, danced a short jig, and said, "And I have something to tell you about what I just overheard in the kitchen."

When he was done, all three went to the screen door to see if they could grab Lily's attention. They wished the telepathic link was still there, but Lily saw them, and quickly got up to let them in. Jack gave her a puzzled look when she sat back down.

"You remember about the Fairies and the Elf?" she asked. Jack nodded his head, his mouth full of pizza. "Well, I just let them in. They're here now, in the kitchen with us." She and Will smiled at each other.

"So I'm the only one that can't see them?"

"For now— but when they realize you'd like to see them, and that you want to thank them, you might suddenly find yourself able to do that," Will said.

Jack picked up his napkin and cleared some crumbs from his lips. "I do thank you all, seen and unseen," he said. "And I think it's time for me to tell the rest of my story."

He told them it began when he was just a young boy, one of two children in a second generation American Jewish family. He'd already told Will how his great-grandparents had managed to flee Germany in time; before their people had lost all their shops and homes; before they were sent off to the camps and certain death. Everyone had been proud of them for realizing they needed to get out in time.

They had come to live with some distant relatives in New York City. But their memories of the family they lost and what had happened back home lived on, and their stories were passed-down. Despite the comfortable life they managed to create in this new world, there was an underlying sense of sadness, helplessness, and mistrust. Jack and his sister seemed to inherit this, too.

When he was twelve, his father was offered a good job in a different place. It was only a few hours away from New York City, and close to Boston, but this smaller Massachusetts town had no other Jews living there at all.

"So you can see why I could really relate to the way Billy felt," Jack continued. "People in the town where we lived were friendly, but I wasn't totally welcome at the homes of school friends. I certainly wasn't allowed to date their sisters. It was hard being an outsider; feeling I was not good enough for them. I couldn't get out of that town fast enough. And I decided that, one day, I would find a way to show them all I was as worthy as they were.

"I was just eighteen, when I made my way back to New York City, and got a job working for a cousin whose company supplies building materials. I applied and was accepted in the night program at a community college. I dated a lot of women there, but found I really couldn't connect with them; not in a meaningful or lasting way."

"I think lots of young people, in all kinds of situations, have the same thing happen to them," Lily offered.

"Yes. Now, I think I understand why," Jack replied. "But at the time, I just kept feeling more and more remote; lost in myself. It was like I had no feelings at all. When I graduated college, I met a guy who told me that building was booming further north on the east coast of Florida—that we should go down there, and with my cousin's backing, get ourselves involved. And that's what we did." He paused and asked Lily for something to drink.

Lily got up and brought Jack a glass of water. Will took this opportunity to close the kitchen door and lower the windows against the increasingly cool night air.

"So, what happened when you got to Florida?" Will asked, sitting back down.

"My partner and I picked the right area and became extremely successful. And I stayed empty inside. It would have gone on like that till the end, if those Fairies hadn't decided they'd had enough of me and worked their magic spell. And if the Fairies from up here…and then Lily…hadn't agreed to help…," he stopped here, too full of emotion to speak.

Lily put her hand over his. At her touch, he calmed down. Taking a deep breath, he went on. "And so, it's different now. I can feel—and a lot of what I feel is good. And what I want to do now is something that will help all of you up here. And especially young people like Billy. Not just because I'm grateful, but because I understand."

"Well, I have to say I'm impressed with how you can see all this—and I guess now you realize there's more to life," Will said.

"I'm surprised, but glad to say, I do," he said. And then, he finished his water, and began to outline his plan.

It started with the purchase of all the land on this mountaintop that he could possibly obtain. Then he would apply to have the woods up behind Will's home designated as a Wildlife Sanctuary. He said he wanted to help make some repairs and upgrades to this house, and make any additions Will might think were necessary, so the whole family could live there. And then he wanted to help fund an education project; including some buildings where crafts were taught, and areas of the land where instruction would be given on how to live in harmony with nature, in an experiential setting.

The Greatest Enchantment

Will and Lily watched Jack's face glowing more and more as he talked about this project. They were all smiles, too, and Runawind was doing his cartwheels in the air to Melarose's giggles. Only Plenty, who was standing next to Will, was quiet. He pulled on Will's sleeve and motioned for him to lean down and listen to what he had to say.

"It sure is wonderful, Will," Plenty began. "And I believe he is sincere, too. Of course, there's still the land, the people, and the creatures to be asking for their blessing, before any of it is done." Plenty waited till Will nodded his assent. "But the most important question of all, must still be asked here. Wait a little while, but don't forget to ask it before you all leave this table tonight."

Will looked confused.

"Oh, don't worry. You will know what it is when the time is right. Just remember what I said. And I wouldn't mind a bit of that left-over cake I heard about, either." With that, the Elf exploded in a belly laugh that left him on his back, on the ground; legs kicking happily at the air.

"Is something wrong?" Jack asked.

"No. It's just the Elf. They have a teasing way of suggesting there are important things to do that you must then figure out on your own."

Jack looked at Lily. "So he is like Rumple..."

"Shhhh! I wouldn't say that name around here if I were you," she laughed. "Even an Elf can suffer from a negative stereotype."

Jack had to laugh, too. "You got me there. You told me he's called 'Plenty', and he's been here for a long time, right?"

"Yes. And he did a lot to create our journey today," Will said.

"Well, whatever you did, Mr. Plenty," Jack said, looking at an area near Will's side. "I want to thank you."

Plenty bounded up from the floor and did a deep bow to the man who couldn't see him. That he thought doing so was hysterical, was plain to see, by those who could.

"Is there any way Jack can see you all now without being in a deep enchantment?" Lily asked. "I'm sure he'd like to be able to remember Melarose and Runawind, and to meet you, too, Plenty."

"Hmmm, I'll have to think about that," Plenty said, stroking his beard.

In the meantime, Will returned to his conversation with Jack. "Where are your parents now—and your sister?"

"Mother passed away a few years ago. I had bought them a condo on the beach, but once Mom was gone, my father said it was too lonely there. He decided to move back to New York City, to be near the rest of the family." Jack sighed. "I wasn't very good at seeing them, I admit. My sister married a guy she met in college. His family owns a vineyard in Napa, so they live out there now. They have two kids. I haven't seen them in years, either." Jack's glow was fading as he spoke these words.

"My boys also thought they'd be better off away from here," Will said. "One day they'll realize it isn't the place, it's what's inside themselves that makes them who they are. I know they need to have their own lives and figure it all out for themselves, but I do miss them— especially how we used to play those instruments together. The ones you saw in the dining room."

"I should probably pay my family a visit," Jack said.

"I'm sure you will. But I guess you'll have to get back down to Florida sometime," Will suggested. "You'll need to see how you feel about things once you're back down there. And there are business decisions to be made, I'm sure."

"Yes, that's true. It's hard to think about that, but I'll have to," Jack said, his happy glow now completely gone.

"It'll be okay. First, you'll have some more time to be up here, and I'd like you to be a part of getting us ready for a ceremony my mother asked me to do." Will said.

Jack brightened again. "I'd be honored."

"What's that?" Lily asked.

"Mom wants me to build a lodge up here, so we can honor the Rock Nation and get their teachings. I know she's right. And she's gone to the trouble of getting permission to build it from some of the Elders." He paused. "She actually did that a few months ago. I guess she had one of her dreams."

"Jack, you may have heard of this. It's called a Sweat Lodge?" Lily asked. "They have them in Florida, too."

Jack shook his head. "I don't think so."

"Well, one day you'll find out why it's got that name," Will said, and laughed. "Tomorrow, we'll scout out the right place to build it, and I'll tell you all about it then."

Looking across the table at Lily, Will saw that she seemed exhausted, and he could tell her mind was working on some perplexing problem. He felt Plenty tug at his sleeve again.

"I'll get the kitchen cleaned up," Will said. "Why don't you two take a walk and see if the moon is up yet. By the way, Jack, do you expect to take Lily back down to Florida with you when you go?"

His question startled them both. Lily said nothing, so Jack answered. "I hadn't really thought about it. I guess— if she wants to come?"

"Well, you two figure it out," Will said, and started clearing the plates.

Outside, the air was crisp and a lopsided moon lingered above the tree line. It was growing toward the full phase; when things come to fruition, energy is high and the bright light helps people see what they're doing and where they're headed, in more ways than one.

Lily suggested going to the front of the house, where they could watch the mountains in the moonlight. When they got there, they stood quietly for a while, gazing west. A few tiny, golden lights came from houses, nestled on the mountainsides; but mostly it was just the deep-blue, star-filled sky above the deeper-blue of the rolling mountain peaks; their patches of rocky clearings, shining, like silver.

"I don't think I'd ever get tired of seeing these mountains in all their changing moods," Jack said.

"I never appreciated it as much as I do now," Lily replied, unconsciously fingering the wooden acorn in her pocket. "If it hadn't been for you, Jack, I might never have gotten the courage to come back here, and then I would have missed being able to see all this, and be with my family again. I know we are all grateful to you for that, even without the ideas you have for this wonderful project. So please don't feel you have to do any more for us than you already have."

"Thanks, Lily. It's hard for me to see our journey here that way, though." He laughed. "But please don't think I feel like I have to do something, or that it's a burden or obligation in my mind. I really want to do this, and I feel happy whenever I think about it. This place is really special, Lily, and I want to help keep it that way."

"You know, in my Spirit Journey today, my Guide told me all of this had been part of a design—even Melarose and Runawind, making the journey down and finding you and Arnold," Lily told him.

"Arnold?" Jack asked.

"Well, I can see why you might not remember him." Lily laughed. "He was one of the Fairies who live near you down there, but not one of those who created the enchantment."

"Arnold. Funny name for a Fairy, isn't it?"

"Well, if you ever see him again, you'll know how unusual he is in every way," Lily said. "And you might see him, too, when you get back home."

"Home," Jack said and sighed. "You know, what your Uncle said back there made me think. The old me of just a few days ago, would have said, yes, I'm taking Lily back with me—but it would have been for my sake, because I was afraid to face it without someone to help me get through the tough things I might have to deal with down there. Not just my business partner, but what that whole lifestyle meant to me; what it brought out in me."

"But now?" Lily asked.

"Now, well, I can see how happy you are here. Somehow, I can feel your full being is in this place." He paused and let out a deep sigh. "And now I can also see that, no matter how grateful I am for what you've done, no matter how that's helped me open my heart to you, Danny's the man you should be with. And you should stay here."

"And what about me—what about how I feel?" Lily said, making him look her in the eyes.

The Greatest Enchantment

"You know I'm right. It makes you feel good to help people and that's a beautiful part of who you are. But you need to develop your own life, and be with a man who supports that, and has the same dreams you do. You might be happy back down there with me for a while, but it wouldn't last. Worrying about me and if I'll stay on track would slowly drain you, and you might not even feel it—until one day, when you looked at me, all you'd see was that lizard you had to help."

"Oh, Jack," she began, reaching out for his hand.

"Lily White Dove, you're a beautiful woman in every way. But feeling is new for me. I can't be sure of what love means to me yet. I can see, though, that Danny loves you very much—and with a true heart that has waited years for you to return. He didn't try to follow you; he didn't ask you to make a choice, even now." Lily looked away, eyes cast down, and brimming with tears. "Oh, yes, I know he did things to influence you, of course. He'd have been crazy not to. But he lets you lead. As a man, Lily, I know what that means. It's not weakness, at all—it's a sign of his strength, his caring, and his knowing. He knows you two are meant to be together—and now, so do I."

"It's just that I thought…"

"You thought you'd have to choose between us. Now you don't have to. That's my gift to you, Lily; to you both. And I know we'll all be the very best of friends." He squeezed her hand between his. "I also know that, when you wake up tomorrow, you'll be happier than you've been in ages. A beautiful life is unfolding for you. I will be so happy to see that happen."

As he said those last words, a most amazing thing occurred. He felt a strong, icy tingle in his legs and feet, followed by several popping sounds. "Lily!" he cried. "I think the lizard skin is gone…it's gone. I'm free!"

"Are you sure?"

"I think so, but I'll show you—look," he said, as he confidently kicked off his left loafer and pulled down his sock, where only bare human skin could be seen on his lower leg and foot.

"But I don't understand," Lily said, looking at him with a worried frown. "Didn't the Wizard say that if the lizard skin came back you could never remove it—and if you got enough to turn you back into a lizard, no Wizard on earth could change that?"

"Yes, I think he did," Jack agreed.

Suddenly, with a *whooshing* sound and a flash of light, Incantaro and the Circle of Seven appeared before them. And Jack could see them, too. He could also see Melarose, Runawind, Plenty, and even the three Fairy Messengers, who fluttered above this group, smiling with delight.

"It is true," Incantaro began. "If you sought to turn yourself back into a lizard with your thoughts and acts, no Wizard on earth could help you. And truly, what I and my Circle of Seven did was to give you but a temporary relief, to see what you might do if you had the choice. For only a pure and unselfish Love could heal that serious enchantment; the kind of love you have shown Billy, Will, and especially Lily, today. That is what brings the true healing—the one that can last."

"And it will? Last, I mean?" Jack asked.

"Oh, yes, it will—and effortlessly, too." Incantaro said. "It's quite an interesting thing to us here in the Otherworld; we see that while humans have a huge capacity to love, they can take a very long time to realize and experience this, because they let their fears grow big and block love's light. But once they do, they feel enough love for themselves to lose their sense of fear and the shame that comes with it. And then they always make the right choices—naturally—as you did here, tonight." He turned by way of emphasis to look at the Circle of Seven, who all nodded enthusiastically. "To choose those words and actions that create the highest good for all things, in every situation—it really is a natural instinct, perhaps long buried, but it exists in all of you. We here in the Otherworld wait with great anticipation for the day that has been foretold, when you all awaken to this love. What a great celebration there will be then—in all the realms."

"Am I dreaming?" Jack asked. Tinkling Fairy and bellowing Elf laughter followed his remark.

Will—who had quietly crept up behind them—stepped between Jack and Lily and put an arm around both. "Incantaro," he said. "I'm glad to see you all here, at my home on the mountain."

The Greatest Enchantment

"No more glad than we are to be here with you all, on this happy night," Incantaro replied, with a big smile, and a twinkle in his eyes.

The next morning when Lily woke, she discovered that what Jack had said was true; she felt happier than she ever had before. Somehow, it seemed she had spent the whole night dreaming of being in Danny's arms, talking and laughing. Maybe it wasn't truly a dream, she thought, but something else—maybe it was a visit in spirit. She had a feeling he would be at the house soon, so she got up and dressed with special care.

When she got to the kitchen, she found she was the only one up. She started the coffee and wondered if she should also start making breakfast. But as she opened the refrigerator door, she heard car tires crunching up the drive. Smiling, she stepped outside.

There was no hesitation now when she greeted Danny Two Hawks. She went straight into his arms, and kissed him with a promise that they both felt, all the way to their toes. Then, arms around each other, they headed for the kitchen, to make a breakfast feast, worthy of them all.

A week later, Will and Jack put the finishing touches on the lodge they had created on the edge of Will's property. It wasn't far from where the deer had dropped off Melarose and Runawind on the day they arrived. Danny and Billy were stacking wood logs in a pile nearby.

"Okay, that seems fine," Will said. "When you get back, Jack, we'll hold a special lodge for you."

"It might not be very long before I am back. When I spoke to my partner this morning, he actually seemed interested in this project. He thinks it's a goodwill gesture that can get us lots of PR," Jack said, laughing. "Wait till he hears the other ideas I have for our business."

"Well, you'll do just fine, and whatever smooths the way for you is good," Will said. "Billy, if you want to follow me with my truck, we can get some lunch in Asheville after I drop Jack at the rental car place."

Billy looked like a different boy. His long hair was neatly trimmed and combed, and he stood tall, looking everyone in the eye when he spoke. "That sounds good. I'll tell Grandma," he said and walked back to the house. As he opened the screen door, the Fairies flew out.

Heading toward the big oak tree, Melarose called to the Elf, who was eating what was left of the breakfast Spirit Plate. "Plenty—it seems we'll be leaving today."

"Oh, I'll be sorry to see you go," Plenty said, making sure to pick up the last tiny piece of bacon, so a sly crow wouldn't grab it while his attention was elsewhere.

"We're so glad we met you," Runawind said. "And we're looking forward happily to the day we'll meet again."

"Well, now, you know I never leave this mountain. They couldn't do without me here." Plenty laughed, and danced a sprightly jig. "So it's you who'll have to return, if it's me you want to see."

"Lily and Danny promised to come get us, so we can be here in time for the wedding. And the way things look, that could be soon," Melarose said, breaking into giggles that made her auburn curls bounce. "The waves of energy that flow when either of them speaks, turns a darker shade of pink each day."

"I do believe you're right. And so we'll part for just the briefest of times in this human world," he said. Satisfied that this was so, Plenty did what all good Elves do—he broke into another song. "Hey ya hi ya, hey yi yo. To a wedding we will go. Hey ya hi ya, hey hi yay. We will bless them on their day; here where Love now leads the way. Hey ya hi ya, hey hi yay."

And as his song went on and on, Melarose and Runawind held hands and flew off to tell Lily they were ready for the trip back to Grandfather Mountain. They could hardly contain their excitement, just thinking about all the stories they would tell—especially the one about their role in the greatest of enchantments. They might even teach some new mountain songs to their Fairy Family. And they knew they'd definitely have a most memorable night in the Fairy Ring, when they were home again, at last.

AUTHOR'S NOTE

When I began writing this story, the idea of Native American characters was not in my mind. It came about naturally, as the story progressed. I am not blessed with Native American ancestors (I did have my DNA checked, just in case, but not a trace appeared). My background is predominantly UK (English, Welsh, Scottish) and Eastern European Jewish.* However, I am a person who has been lucky enough to receive some instruction from teachers of various Native American traditions—mainly Lakota, but also Cherokee and Seneca. Their teachings enriched my life in more ways than I can express. But, I want to make it clear that I do not consider myself, or pretend to be a spokesman for the rich and varied culture of Native Americans.

I am also aware of the sensitivity of this culture and honor their reasons for continuing to keep many of their practices secret. It may surprise some 21st Century readers that, until fairly recently, the American Indians (as they were then called) were prosecuted for practicing their spiritual ceremonies or using their religious objects—many of which are now the property of collectors and museums. In fact, it was not until President Jimmy Carter signed the American Indian Religious Freedom Act in August of 1978,** that Native Americans were allowed free access to their own religious sites, objects, and ceremonies. Before this, these American citizens were denied their First Amendment right of "free exercise" of religion. Therefore, along with other abuses suffered during English and European colonization of the Americas (including being marched on foot from the mountains of the Carolinas to Oklahoma Reservations, on what has come to be known as The Trail of Tears that is mentioned in this book), it is not hard to understand why these people tend to reject the idea of outsiders coming too close to their sacred practices now.

When this Forest Fairy Adventure was complete, I asked Amy Sindersine, a person with Native American ancestry and a member of Reedy River Intertribal Association in Gray Court, SC, if I could read her the passages that describe my Native American characters and the ceremonial practices they perform. I wanted to be sure I was both accurate and not overstepping any sensitive boundaries. Fortunately, Amy was pleased with what she heard—both the information contained and the way it is conveyed. I am very grateful to her for this approval.

If this book in any small way uplifts or enhances the experience of the Native American people in the Carolinas, or anywhere else, I will be both happy and humbled at the mysterious way Spirit works for good.

Shellie Enteen
Greer, SC
August 2015

For more information about Cherokee, NC, please go to http://visitcherokeenc.com

*The fact that there is one Jewish character in the story also came as a surprise, but it allows me to bring in a message that could be helpful to everyone. My portrayal of this character's background comes from the family stories of close friends I had while growing up in New York City, many of whom had parents or grandparents who were fortunate enough to leave Europe in the late 1930s. My own Jewish relatives emigrated from Russia, arriving in NYC before 1900.

** An interesting fact about the American Indian Religious Freedom Act Religion Act is that it was introduced in 1977 by James George Abourezk, the first Greek Orthodox Christian of Lebanese-Antiochite descent to serve in the United States Senate. He represented South Dakota from 1973 until 1979.

The ancient city of Antioch was one of four "sister cities" in northwestern Syria, founded after the death of Alexander the Great. It was populated by peoples from the surrounding regions, and immigrating Jews were given full status from the start. It seems possible that the ancestral memory of religious tolerance was passed down to this man, who represented the state that holds the Reservations of the Lakota people, and their sacred Black Hills.

Let us hope that tolerance will one day be the natural state for us all.

Printed in the United States
By Bookmasters